The
ESSENTIAL C

The
ESSENTIAL COLLECTION

#1 *New York Times* Bestselling Author

DEBBIE MACOMBER

BRIDE on the Loose

◆ **HARLEQUIN**®
™ESSENTIAL DEBBIE MACOMBER COLLECTION

Recycling programs
for this product may
not exist in your area.

ISBN-13: 978-0-373-47295-6

BRIDE ON THE LOOSE

Copyright © 1992 by Debbie Macomber

For questions and comments about the quality of this book, please contact us at CustomerService@Harlequin.com.

Printed in U.S.A.

DEBBIE MACOMBER

is a number one *New York Times* and *USA TODAY* best-selling author. Her books include *1225 Christmas Tree Lane*, *1105 Yakima Street*, *A Turn in the Road*, *Hannah's List* and *Debbie Macomber's Christmas Cookbook*, as well as *Twenty Wishes*, *Summer on Blossom Street* and *Call Me Mrs. Miracle*. She has become a leading voice in women's fiction worldwide and her work has appeared on every major bestseller list, including those of the *New York Times*, *USA TODAY*, *Publishers Weekly* and *Entertainment Weekly*. She is a multiple award winner, and won the 2005 Quill Award for Best Romance. There are more than one hundred million copies of her books in print. Two of her Harlequin MIRA Christmas titles have been made into Hallmark Channel Original Movies, and the Hallmark Channel has launched a series based on her bestselling Cedar Cove series. For more information on Debbie and her books, visit her website, www.debbiemacomber.com.

To Virginia and Dean,
whose many years of love have inspired me.

One

It was one of those days. Jason Manning scrubbed his hands in the stainless-steel sink, then applied ointment to several scratches. He'd just finished examining and prescribing antibiotics for a feisty Persian cat with a bladder infection. The usually ill-mannered feline had never been his most cooperative patient, but today she'd taken a particular dislike to Jason.

He left the examining room and was greeted by Stella, his receptionist, who steered him toward his office. She wore a suspiciously silly grin, as if to say "this should be interesting."

"There's a young lady who'd like a few minutes with you," was all the information she'd give him. Her cryptic message didn't please him any more than the Persian's blatant distaste for him had.

Curious, Jason moved into his book-lined office. "Hello," he said in the friendliest voice he could muster.

"Hi." A teenage girl who seemed vaguely familiar stood as he entered the room. She glanced nervously in his direction as if he should recognize her. When it was obvious he didn't, she introduced herself. "I'm Carrie Weston." She paused, waiting expectantly.

"Hello, Carrie," Jason said. He'd seen her around, but for the life of him, couldn't recall where. "How can I help you?"

"You don't remember me, do you?"

"Ah...no." He couldn't see any point in pretending. If a cat could outsmart him, he was fair game for a teenager.

"We're neighbors. My mom and I live in the same apartment complex as you."

He did his best to smile and nod as though he'd immediately placed her, but he hadn't. He racked his brain trying to recall which apartment was hers. Although he owned and managed the building, Jason didn't interact much with his tenants. He was careful to choose renters who cared about their privacy as much as he cared about his. He rarely saw any of them other than to collect the rent, and even then most just slipped their checks under his door around the first of the month.

Carrie sat back down, her hands clenched tightly in her lap. "I—I'm sorry to bother you, but I've been trying to talk to you for some time, and...and this seemed to be the only way I could do it without my mother finding out."

"Your mother?"

"Charlotte Weston. We live in 1-A."

Jason nodded. The Westons had been in the apartment for more than a year. Other than when they'd signed the rental agreement, Jason couldn't recall speaking to either the mother or her daughter.

"Is there a problem?"

"Not a problem...exactly." Carrie stood once again and opened her purse, taking out a thin wad of bills, which she leafed through and counted slowly. When she'd finished, she looked up at him. "It's my mother," she announced.

"Yes?" Jason prompted. He didn't have a clue where this conversation was leading or how long it would take the girl to get there. Stella knew he had a terrier waiting, yet she'd purposely routed him into his office.

"She needs a man," Carrie said, squaring her shoulders.

"I beg your pardon?" The girl had his attention now.

"My mother needs a man. I'm here to offer you one hundred dollars if you'll take her out on a date. You are single, aren't you?"

"Yes…but…" Jason was so surprised, he answered without thinking. Frankly, he didn't know whether to ask which of his brothers had put her up to this, or simply to laugh outright. He couldn't very well claim he'd never been propositioned before, but this was by far the most original instance he'd encountered in thirty-odd years.

"She's not ugly or anything."

"Ah…I'm not sure what to tell you." The girl was staring at him so candidly, so forthrightly, Jason realized within seconds it was no joke.

"I don't think my mother's happy."

Jason leaned against the side of his oak desk and crossed his arms. "Why would you assume my taking her out will make a difference?"

"I…don't know. I'm just hoping. You see, my mom and dad got divorced when I was little. I don't remember my dad, and apparently he doesn't remember me, either, because I've never heard from him. Mom doesn't say much about what went wrong, but it must've been bad because she never dates. I didn't care about that before, only now..."

"Only now what?" Jason asked when she hesitated.

"I want to start dating myself, and my mother's going totally weird on me. She says I'm too young. Boy, is she out of it! I'm not allowed to date until I'm sixteen. Can you imagine anything so ridiculous?"

"Uhh..." Jason wasn't interested in getting involved in a mother-daughter squabble. "Not being a father myself, I can't really say."

"The ninth-grade dance is coming up in a few weeks and I want to go."

"Your mother won't allow you to attend the dance?" That sounded a bit harsh to Jason, but as he'd just stated, he wasn't in a position to know.

"Oh, she'll let me go, except she intends to drop me off and pick me up when the dance is over."

"And that's unacceptable?"

"Of course it is! It's—it's the most awful thing she could do to me. I'd be mortified to have my mother waiting in the school parking lot to take me home after the dance. I'd be humiliated in front of my friends. You've just got to help me." A note of desperation raised her voice on the last few words.

"I don't understand what you want me to do," Jason hedged. He couldn't see any connection between Carrie's attending the all-important ninth-grade dance and him wining and dining her mother.

"You need me to spell it out for you?" Carrie's eyes were wide, her gaze scanning the room. "I'm offering you serious money to seduce my mother."

For a wild instant, Jason thought he hadn't heard her right. "Seduce her?"

"My mother's practically a virgin all over again. She needs a man."

"You're sure about this?" Jason was having a hard time keeping a straight face. He could hardly wait to tell his brother Rich. The two of them would have a good laugh over it.

"Absolutely positive." Carrie didn't even flinch. Her expression grew more confident. "Mom's forgotten what it's like to be in love. All she thinks about is work. Don't get me wrong... My mother's an awesome person, but she's so prim and proper...and stubborn. What she really needs is...well, you know."

Jason felt sorry for the kid, but he didn't see how he could help her. Now that he thought about it, he did recall what Charlotte Weston looked like. In fact, he could remember the day she'd moved in. She'd seemed feminine and attractive, more than a little intriguing. But he'd noticed a guardedness, too, that sent an unmistakable signal. He'd walked away with the impression that she was as straitlaced as a nun and about as warm and inviting as an Alaskan winter.

"Why me?" Jason was curious enough to wonder why Carrie had sought *him* out. Apparently his charisma was more alluring than he'd realized.

"Well, because...just because, that's all," Carrie answered with perfect teenage logic. "And I figured I wouldn't have to pay you as much as I would one of those dating services. You seem nice." She gnawed on her lower lip. "Being a veterinarian is good, too."

"How's that?"

"You've probably had lots of experience soothing injured animals, and I think my mother's going to need some of that—comforting and reassuring, you know?" The girl's voice became fervent. "She's been hurt.... She doesn't talk about it, but she loved my father and I think she must be afraid of falling in love again. I even think she might like another baby someday." This last bit of information was clearly an afterthought. Carrie cast him a speculative glance to be sure she hadn't said something she shouldn't have. "Don't worry about that—she's probably too old anyway," she added quickly.

"She wants a baby?" Jason could feel the hair on the back of his neck rising. This woman-child was leading him toward quicksand, and he was going to put a stop to it right now.

"No--no...I mean, she's never said so, but I saw her the other day holding a friend's newborn and she had that look in her eyes... I thought she was going to cry." She paused. "I shouldn't have said anything."

For one brief, insane moment, Jason had actually considered the challenge of seducing Charlotte Weston, but the mention of a baby brought him solidly back to earth.

"Listen, Carrie," Jason said, "I'm sorry, but this isn't going to work."

"It's got to," she pleaded urgently, "just for one date. Couldn't you ask her out? Just once? If you don't, I'll be humiliated in front of my entire class. I'd rather not even go to the dance if my mother drives me."

Jason hated to disappoint her, but he couldn't see himself in the role of rescuing a fifteen-year-old damsel in distress from her mother's heavy hand, even if Carrie did make a halfway decent case.

"Is it the money?" Carrie asked, her eyes imploring. "I might be able to scrounge up another twenty dollars...but I'm going to need some cash for the dance."

"It isn't the money," Jason assured her.

Wearing a dejected look, Carrie stood. "You sure you don't want to take a couple of days to think it over?"

"I'm sure."

She released a long, frustrated sigh. "I was afraid you were going to say that."

"Good luck." Jason held open the door. He had no intention of asking Charlotte Weston out on a date, but he he did feel sorry for Carrie. Although he hadn't been a teenager in years, he hadn't forgotten how important these things could seem. Things like the ninth-grade dance.

Charlotte let herself into the apartment at six that evening. She slipped off her heels and rubbed the tense muscles at the back of her neck.

"Hi, Mom," Carrie called cheerfully from the kitchen. "How was work?"

"Fine." There was no need to burden her daughter with how terrible her day had been. Her job as an executive assistant at a large insurance agency might have sounded high-powered and influential, but in reality it was neither. Charlotte worked long hours with little appreciation or reward. For six months, ever since Harry Ward had taken over as managing director, she'd been telling herself it was time to change jobs. But she couldn't give up the security of her position, no matter how much she disliked her boss.

"How was school?" she asked.

"Good. Tickets for the dance went on sale today." Her daughter looked hopefully at Charlotte, as though expecting her to make some profound comment.

Charlotte chose to ignore the pointed stare. Her stand on the dance issue was causing a strain in their relationship, but she refused to give in to her daughter's pressure. Carrie wasn't going on an actual *date*. She was interested in a boy named Brad, but as far as Charlotte was concerned, Carrie could attend the dance with her girlfriends and meet him there. Good grief, the girl was only fifteen!

"Mom, can we *please* talk about the dance?"

"Of course, but…"

"You're not going to change your mind, right?" Carrie guessed, then sighed. "What can I say to prove how unreasonable you're being? Every girl in my class is going to the dance with a *boy*. And Brad *asked* me."

Charlotte reached for an apron, tied it about her waist and opened the refrigerator door. She took out a package of ground turkey for taco salad. She wasn't up to another round of arguments over the dance.

"Did you buy a dance ticket?" Charlotte asked, forcing an artificial lightness into her voice.

"No. I won't, either. I'd rather sit home for the rest of my life than have my *mother* drop me off and pick me up. Brad's father said he'd drive us both… What am I supposed to tell Brad? That my mother doesn't trust his father's driving? You're making way too big a deal out of this."

Ah, the certainty of youth, Charlotte mused.

"Will you think about it?" Carrie implored. "Please?"

"All right," Charlotte promised. She hated to be so hardheaded, but when it came to her daughter, she found little room for compromise. To her way of thinking, Carrie was too young for a real date, even if the boy in question wasn't the one driving.

The meat was simmering in the cast-iron skillet as Charlotte started to wash the lettuce. The faucet came off in her hand, squirting icy water toward the ceiling, and she gasped.

"What's wrong?" Carrie asked, leaping up from the kitchen table where she was doing her homework.

"The faucet broke!" Already Charlotte was down on her knees, her head under the sink, searching for the valve to cut off the water supply.

"There's water everywhere," Carrie shrieked.

"I know." Most of it had landed on Charlotte.

"Are you going to be able to fix it?" Carrie asked anxiously.

Charlotte sat on the floor, her back against the lower cupboards, her knees under her chin. This was all she needed to make her day complete. "I don't know," she muttered, pushing damp hair away from her face with both hands. "But it shouldn't be that hard."

"You should call the apartment manager," Carrie said. "You've had to work all day. If something breaks down, he should be the one to fix it, not you. We don't know anything about faucets. We're helpless."

"Helpless?" Charlotte raised her eyebrows at that. The two of them had dealt with far more difficult problems over the years. By comparison, a broken faucet was nothing. "I think we can handle it."

"Of course we can, but why should we?" Carrie demanded. "We pay our rent on time every month. The least the manager could do is see to minor repairs. He should fix them right away, too." She marched over to the wall phone and yanked the receiver from the hook. "Here," she said dramatically. "You call him."

"I...I don't know the number." They'd lived in the apartment for well over a year and until now there hadn't been any reason to contact the manager.

"It's around here somewhere," Carrie said, pulling open the top kitchen drawer and riffling through the phone book and some other papers. Within a very brief time, she'd located the phone number. "His name is Jason Manning. He's a veterinarian."

"He's a vet? I didn't realize that." But then, Charlotte had only met the man once, and their entire conversation had been about the apartment. He seemed pleasant enough. She'd seen him in the parking lot a few times and he struck her as an overgrown kid. Frankly, she was surprised to learn he was a veterinarian, since she'd never seen him in anything other than a baseball cap, jeans and a T-shirt. Dressing up for him was a pair of jeans that weren't torn or stained and a sweatshirt.

"Are you going to phone him?" Carrie asked, holding out the receiver.

"I suppose I will." Charlotte rose awkwardly to her feet in her straight skirt. By the time she was upright, her daughter had dialed the number and handed her the receiver.

"Hello," came Jason Manning's voice after the first ring, catching her off guard.

"Oh...hello... This is Charlotte Weston in apartment 1-A. We have a broken faucet. I managed to turn off the valve, but we'd appreciate having it repaired as quickly as possible."

"A broken faucet," he repeated, and although she knew it made no sense, he sounded suspicious to Charlotte, as though he thought she'd purposely interrupted his evening. She resented his attitude.

"Yes, a broken faucet," she returned stiffly. "It came off in my hand when I went to wash some lettuce. There's water everywhere." A slight exaggeration, but a necessary one. "If you'd prefer, I can contact a plumber. Naturally there'll be an additional charge for repairs this late in the day."

He muttered something Charlotte couldn't decipher, then said, "I'll be right over." He didn't seem too pleased, but that was his problem. He shouldn't have agreed to manage the apartments if he wasn't willing to deal with the hassles that went along with the job.

"What did he say?" her daughter asked, eyes curious, when Charlotte hung up the phone. "Is he coming?"

"He said he'd be right over."

"Good." Carrie studied her critically. "You might want to change clothes."

"Change clothes? Whatever for?" Surprised at her daughter's concern, Charlotte glanced down at her business suit. She didn't see anything wrong with it other than a little water, and in any event, she couldn't care less about impressing the apartment manager.

"Whatever." Carrie rolled her eyes, returning to her homework. No sooner had she sat down than the doorbell chimed. Her daughter leapt suddenly to her feet as if she expected to find a rock star at the door. "I'll get it!"

Jason considered the whole thing a nuisance call. It didn't take a rocket scientist to figure out what Carrie Weston was doing. The girl had arranged this broken faucet just so he'd have a chance to see Charlotte. The kid seemed to think that once Jason got a good look at her mother, he'd change his mind about wanting to date her. Well, there wasn't much chance of that.

Apparently the girl thought he was something of a player. Jason might've gotten a kick out of that a few years ago, but not now. Not when he was nearing middle age. These days he was more concerned about his cholesterol level and his weight than with seducing a reluctant woman.

He probably would've ended up getting married if things had worked out between him and Julie, but they hadn't. She'd been with Charlie nearly seven years now, and the last he'd heard, she had three kids. He wished her and her husband well, and suffered no regrets. Sure, it had hurt when they'd broken off their relationship, but in the end it just wasn't meant to be. He was pragmatic enough to accept that and go on with his life.

Jason enjoyed the company of women as much as any man did, but he didn't like the fact that they all wanted to reform him. He was disorganized, slovenly and a sports nut. Women didn't appreciate those qualities in a man. They would smile sweetly, claim they loved him just the way he was and then try to change him. The problem was, Jason didn't want to be refined, reformed or domesticated.

Charlotte Weston was a prime example of the type of woman he particularly avoided. Haughty. Dignified. Proper. She actually washed lettuce. Furthermore, she made a point of letting him know it.

"Hi." Carrie opened the door for him, grinning from ear to ear.

"The faucet broke?" Jason didn't bother to keep the sarcasm out of his voice.

She nodded, her smile as sly as a wink. "Kind of accidentally on purpose," she explained under her breath.

Jason was surprised she'd admit as much. "I thought that might be the case."

She pulled a screw from the small front

pocket of her jeans and handed it to him. "It was the only way I could think of to get you here to see my mother up close—only don't be obvious about it, all right?"

"Carrie, is it the apartment manager?" The subject of their discussion walked into the living room, drying her hands on a terry-cloth apron.

Not bad was Jason's first reaction. She'd changed her hair since the last time he'd seen her; it was a cloud of disarrayed brown curls instead of the chignon she'd worn a year earlier. The curls gave her a softer, more feminine appeal. She was good-looking, too, not trying-to-make-an-impression gorgeous, but attractive in a modest sort of way. Her eyes were a deep shade of blue, as blue as his own. They were also intense and…sad, as though she'd withstood more than her share of problems over the years. But then, who hadn't?

Her legs were attractive, too. Long and slender. She was tall—easily five-eight, maybe five-nine.

"She's not bad-looking, is she?" Carrie asked in a whisper.

"Shh." Jason slid back a warning.

"Mom, this is Dr. Jason Manning, remember? Our apartment manager," Carrie said, her arm making a sweeping gesture toward her mother.

"Hello." She stayed where she was, her fingers still clutching the apron.

"Hi. You called about the broken faucet?" He took a couple of steps into the room, carrying his tool kit. He'd have a talk with Carrie later. If this took more than a few minutes, he might be late for the Lakers play-off game. It was the fifth game in the series, and Jason had no intention of missing it.

"The broken faucet's in the kitchen," Charlotte said, leading the way.

"This shouldn't take long." Jason set his tools on the counter and reached for the disconnected faucet. "Looks like it might be missing a screw." He turned pointedly to Carrie, then made a show of sorting through his tool kit. "My guess is that I have an identical one in here." He pretended to find the screw Carrie had handed him, then held it up so they could all examine it. "Ah, here's one now."

"Don't be so obvious about it," Carrie warned in a heated whisper. "I don't want Mom to know."

Charlotte seemed oblivious to the undercurrents passing between him and Carrie, which was probably just as well. He'd let the kid get away with it this time, but he wasn't coming back for any repeat performances of this handyman routine.

"I should have this fixed in a couple of minutes," he said.

"Take your time," Carrie told him. "No need to rush." She walked up behind Jason and whispered, "Give her a chance, will you?"

True to his word, it took Jason all of thirty seconds to make the necessary repair.

"The bathroom faucet's been leaking, hasn't it, Mom? Don't you think we should have him look at that, too, while he's here?"

Jason glanced at his watch and frowned. If the kid kept this up, he'd miss the start of the basketball game. But he decided he had little choice: pay now or pay later. He gave Carrie the lead she was hoping for. "Or it'll need fixing tomorrow, right?"

"Probably." There was a clear glint of warning in the fifteen-year-old's eyes.

Charlotte turned around and glanced from one to the other. Crossing her arms, she studied her daughter, then looked at Jason as if seeing him for the first time. Really seeing him. Apparently she didn't like what she saw.

"Is something going on here I don't know about?" she asked.

"What makes you say that?" Carrie said with wide-eyed innocence.

Jason had to hand it to the girl; she had the look down to an art form.

"Just answer the question, Caroline Marie."

The mother wasn't a slacker in "the look" department, either. She had eyes that would flash freeze a pot of boiling water.

The girl held her own for an admirable length of time before caving in to the icy glare. She lifted her shoulders with an expressive sigh and said, "If you must know, I took the screw out of the faucet so we'd have to call Jason over here."

Once again Jason glanced at his watch, hoping to extract himself from their discussion. This was between mother and daughter—not mother, daughter and innocent bystander. He hadn't meant to let Charlotte in on her daughter's scheme, but neither was he willing to become a full-time pawn in Carrie's little games. No telling how many other repair projects the girl might turn up for him.

"Why would you want Dr. Manning here?" Charlotte asked with a frown.

"Because he's a good-looking man and he

seems nice and I thought it would be great if you got to know each other."

It was time to make his move, Jason decided. "If you'll excuse me, I'll be leaving now."

"You purposely broke the faucet so we could call him down here?" Charlotte gestured toward Jason.

Carrie sent him an irritated look as though to suggest this was all his fault. "I wanted him to see you. For being thirty-five, you aren't half bad. Once he saw your potential, I was sure he'd ask you out on a date. I tried to talk him into it earlier, but—"

"You *what?*" Charlotte exploded. Color flashed into her cheeks like bright neon lights. Her eyes narrowed. "Tell me you didn't! *Please* tell me you didn't!"

Carrie snapped her mouth shut, about ten seconds too late to suit Jason.

"This is all a big joke, isn't it?" Charlotte turned to Jason for reassurance, which was a mistake, since he was glaring at Carrie, irritated with her for saying far more than necessary.

"I had to do something," Carrie cried, defending herself. "You need a man. I saw the look on your face when you were holding

Kathy Crenshaw's baby. You've never said anything, but you want more children. You never date... I don't know what my father did to you, but you've shut yourself off and—and...I was just trying to help."

Charlotte stalked to the far side of the small kitchen. "I can't *believe* this. You actually asked a man to take me out?"

"I did more than ask. I offered him money!"

Charlotte whirled on Jason. "Just what kind of man are you? Agreeing to my daughter's plans... Why...you're detestable!"

Despite himself, Jason smiled, which was no doubt the worst thing he could have done. "So I've been told. Now if you'll both excuse me, I'll leave you to your discussion."

"What kind of man are you?" Charlotte demanded a second time, following him to the door, blocking his exit.

"Mom..."

"Go to your room, young lady. I'll deal with you later." She pointed the way, as if Carrie needed directions.

Jason hadn't imagined things would go like this, and he did feel badly about it, but that didn't help. Charlotte Weston could think harshly of him if she wanted, but now Car-

rie was in trouble and Jason felt halfway responsible.

"She was just trying to do you a good turn," he said matter-of-factly. "Think of it as an early Mother's Day gift."

Two

With her daughter out of the room, Charlotte scowled at Jason Manning, angrier than she could ever remember being.

"You're…" She couldn't think of anything bad enough to call him.

"*Detestable* is a good word." He was practically laughing at her!

"Detestable," she repeated, clenching her fists. "I'll have you know I'm reporting you to…" The name of the government agency, any government agency, was beyond her.

"Children Protective Services," he supplied.

"Them, too." She jerked the apron from her waist and threw it on the floor. Surprised by her own action, Charlotte tried to steady herself. "According to the terms of our rental agreement, I'm giving you our two-weeks' notice as of this minute. I refuse to live near a man as…"

"Heinous," he offered, looking bored.

"Heinous as you," she stated emphatically. Then with an indignant tilt of her chin, she said as undramatically as she could manage, "Now kindly leave my home."

"As you wish." He opened the door and without a backward glance walked out of her apartment. He'd worn a cocky grin throughout, as if he found her tirade thoroughly amusing.

His attitude infuriated Charlotte. She followed him to the door and loudly turned the lock, hoping the sound of it would echo in his ears for a good long time.

When he'd gone, Charlotte discovered she was shaking so badly she needed to sit down. She sank onto a chair, her knees trembling.

"Mom?" A small voice drifted down from the hallway. "You weren't serious about us moving, were you?"

"You're darn right I'm serious. I'm so serious I'd prefer to live in our car than have anything to do with that…that…apartment manager!"

"But why?" Carrie's voice gained strength as she wandered from her bedroom to the living room, where Charlotte was seated. "Why are we moving?"

Charlotte had clearly failed as a mother. One more layer of guilt to add to all the others. "You mean you honestly don't know?"

"To punish me?" Carrie asked, her eyes brimming with unshed tears. "I'm really sorry, Mom. I didn't mean to embarrass you."

What Carrie had done was bad enough, but Jason Manning was an adult. He should've known better. True, her daughter had played a major role in all this, but Carrie was a child and didn't fully understand what she was suggesting. Her daughter had Charlotte's best interests at heart, misguided though she was.

Jason Manning, on the other hand, had planned to take advantage of them both.

"It isn't you I'm furious with, it's him." Charlotte pointed after Jason. To think a professional man would actually agree to such an idiotic scheme.

"Dr. Manning?"

"The man's a sleaze! Imagine, taking money from you—"

"He didn't."

Charlotte hesitated, the sick feeling in her stomach intensifying. "Of course he did," she argued, "otherwise he wouldn't have played out this ridiculous game with you."

"I was the one who took the screw out of the faucet, Mom. Jason Manning didn't know anything about it. When I asked him if he'd agree to take you out on a date, he refused. He was really nice about it and everything, but he didn't seem to think it was a good idea. That's when I offered him the babysitting money I've been saving, but he wouldn't take it."

A dizziness replaced Charlotte's nausea. Several of Jason's comments suddenly made sense, especially the hint of sarcasm she'd detected when he'd held up the missing screw. Yet he'd allowed her to rant at him, not even bothering to defend himself.

"But…"

"You really aren't going to make us move, are you?"

Charlotte closed her eyes and groaned. She'd had a rotten day at the office, but misplacing a file and getting yelled at in front of an important client didn't compare with the humiliation that had been awaiting her at home.

"I wonder how many fat grams there are in crow," she muttered under her breath.

"Fat grams in crow? Are you all right, Mom?"

"I'm going to be eating a huge serving of it," Charlotte grumbled, and she had the distinct feeling she wasn't going to enjoy the experience.

She gave herself an hour. Sixty minutes to calm her nerves, have dinner and wipe down the counters while Carrie loaded the dishwasher. Sixty minutes to figure out how she was going to take back her two-weeks' notice.

"You're going to talk to him, aren't you?" Carrie prodded her. "Right away."

Charlotte didn't need Carrie to identify *him*. They both had only one *him* on their minds.

"I'll talk to him."

"Thank heaven." Carrie sighed with relief.

"But when I finish with Jason Manning, you and I are going to sit down and have a serious discussion, young lady."

Some of the enthusiasm left Carrie's pretty blue eyes as she nodded reluctantly.

Charlotte would've preferred to delay the apology, but the longer she put it off, the more difficult it would become.

Her steps were hesitant as she approached

Jason's apartment. For some reason, she chose to knock instead of pressing the doorbell.

When he didn't answer right away, she assumed, gratefully, that she'd been given a reprieve. Yet, at the same time, she hated letting the situation fester overnight. With reinforced determination, she knocked again.

"Hold your horses," Jason shouted from the other side of the door.

Charlotte took one step in retreat, squared her shoulders and drew in a deep breath. He opened the door. He looked preoccupied and revealed no emotion when he saw her.

"Hello," she said, hating how shaky she sounded. She paused long enough to clear her throat. "Would it be okay if I came inside?"

"Sure." He stepped aside to let her into his apartment. One glance told her he wasn't much of a housekeeper. A week's worth of newspapers were scattered across the carpet. Dirty dishes, presumably from his dinner, sat on the coffee table, along with the remote control, which he picked up. The TV was instantly muted. He walked over to the recliner and removed a pile of clothes, probably things he'd recently taken from the dryer.

"You can sit here," he said, indicating the recliner, his arms full of clothes.

Charlotte smiled and sat down.

"You want a beer?"

"Ah...sure." She didn't normally drink much, but if there was ever a time she needed to fortify her courage, it was now.

Her response seemed to surprise him. It certainly surprised her. He went into the kitchen, returning a moment later with a bottle and a glass. Apparently he found something he didn't like in the glass because he grabbed a dish towel from the stack of clothes he'd dumped on the floor and used it to rub the inside. When he'd finished, he raised the glass to the light for inspection.

"Don't worry about it. I prefer to drink my beer from the bottle."

He nodded, then sat down across from her, leaning back and resting his ankle on his knee. He seemed completely relaxed, as well he should. *He* wasn't the one who'd have to plead temporary insanity.

"It's about what happened earlier," she began, gripping the beer bottle with both hands. "I talked to Carrie and discovered you hadn't exactly, uh, fallen in with her scheme. I'm afraid I assumed you had."

"Don't worry about it. It was a simple misunderstanding."

"I know. Nevertheless..."

"I'll place an ad in the paper for the apartment tomorrow. Would it be okay if I started showing it right away?"

So, he was going to make this difficult after all. "That's another reason I'm here."

"You've changed your mind about moving?" he asked conversationally, his gaze slipping from her to the television screen and back. Charlotte, however, wasn't fooled. Like any other man, he would enjoy watching her squirm.

His eyes wandered back to the silent TV. He made a fist, then jerked his elbow back in a gesture of satisfaction. Obviously things were going well for whichever team he was rooting for—much better than they were for her.

"I'd prefer not to move... Carrie and I like living where we do. The area suits us and, well...to be honest, I spoke in anger." This was all she was willing to give. If he was vindictive enough to demand she vacate the apartment, then so be it. She wasn't going to beg.

"Fine, then." He shrugged. "You're a good tenant and I'd hate to lose you." His gaze didn't waver from the television.

"Who's playing?"

He seemed surprised by her question, as though she should know something so elementary. "The Lakers and the Denver Nuggets."

"Go ahead and turn up the sound if you want."

He frowned. "You don't mind?"

"Of course not. I interrupted your game. If I'd known you were watching it, I would've waited until it was over." She took a swig of beer so he'd realize she intended to be on her way shortly.

He reached for the remote control with an eagerness he didn't bother to disguise. He pushed the volume button, dropped his leg and scooted forward, immediately absorbed in the game.

Charlotte didn't know that much about sports. Generally they bored her, but perhaps that was because she didn't understand the rules. No one had ever taken the time to explain them to her. Football seemed absolutely senseless, and basketball hardly less so.

As far as she could tell, basketball involved a herd of impossibly tall men racing up and down a polished wooden floor, passing a ball back and forth until one of them forged ahead to the basket to try to score. It seemed that whenever the contest became interesting, the referees would blow their whistles and everything would come to a grinding halt. She couldn't understand why the referees chose to wear zebra-striped shirts, either, since it wasn't likely anyone would confuse the short, balding men with the players.

"Who's winning?" That was innocuous enough, she decided. Such a simple question wouldn't reveal the extent of her ignorance.

"For now, the Lakers. They're up by four, but the lead's been changing the entire game."

"Oh." She watched for several minutes, then asked what she considered to be another harmless question. "Why do some throws count for three points and others only two?"

The thoroughness of his response astonished her, prompting several more questions. By the time he'd answered them all, he must've been aware that she barely knew one end of the court from the other. But if he was shocked by her lack of knowledge, he didn't let it show.

Soon Charlotte found herself actually enjoying the game. Now that it made a bit more sense, she began to understand why Jason liked it so much. The score was tied a minute before halftime and when the Lakers scored at the buzzer to take the lead, Charlotte leapt to her feet and cheered.

Jason raised his eyebrows at her display of enthusiasm, which made Charlotte all the more self-conscious. Slowly she lowered herself back into the chair. "Sorry," she mumbled.

"Don't be. I just didn't expect you'd be the type to appreciate sports."

"Generally I'm not. This is the first time I've had any idea what was going on."

A patronizing smile flashed in and out of his eyes. But that one instant was enough. Charlotte recognized the look; she'd seen other men wear the same expression. Men seemed to assume that because they could change their own oil and hook up a TV by themselves, they were naturally superior to women. Charlotte had run into that attitude most of her life.

Since it was her duty to defend womankind, and because she'd been fortified with a beer, Charlotte jumped to her feet. "Don't get haughty with me, Jason Manning!" she said.

Trying to recover her dignity, she sat back down, tucking one leg beneath her. "You think just because you happen to know a few sports rules, men are superior to women."

"We are," he returned wholeheartedly, without the least bit of reservation.

Charlotte laughed. "At least you're honest. I'm sick of men who pay lip service to women, then go into the men's room and snicker behind our backs."

"I'm honest to a fault," Jason agreed. "I'm willing to snicker right in front of you."

"Somehow I don't find that much of a compliment."

"Hey, admit it. Men *are* superior, and if you haven't owned up to it by now, you should. Don't forget, God created us first."

"Give me a break," Charlotte said, rolling her eyes.

"All right. If you can, name one thing a woman does better than a man, other than having babies, which is a given."

"I'll improve on that. I'll name…several."

"Several? You won't be able to come up with one."

"Okay, then," Charlotte said, accepting his challenge. "Women are more sensitive than men. Really," she added when he snorted in response.

"Sure, you cry in movies. That negates your whole argument."

"I'm not talking about crying." She frowned at him. "I'm referring to feelings! Women aren't afraid to face their feelings. Men are so terrified of emotion they hold it inside until they're totally bent out of shape."

Jason laughed, although grudgingly. "I suppose you think women are smarter than men, too."

"No," she said sincerely. "I'd say we're about even in that department."

"Go on," he urged, as though he suspected she'd depleted her list.

"Another thing. Women are better at multi-tasking than men. We're used to juggling all kinds of responsibilities."

Jason snickered.

"I'm serious," she returned. "If you think about it, you'll realize it's true. Women are expected to help support the family financially. Not only that, we're *also* expected to assume the role of emotional caretaker. Responsibility for the family falls on the woman's shoulders, not the man's. Have you ever noticed how rarely men put the needs of others before their own?"

"'Needs,'" Jason echoed. "Good grief, what's *that?* Some pop-psych buzzword."

Charlotte ignored him. "Frankly, I feel sorry for you guys. You've been allowed to remain children most of your lives. You've never been given the chance to grow up."

Jason looked as though he wanted to argue with her, but couldn't come up with an adequate rebuttal.

"Women handle pain better than men, too." Charlotte was on a roll. "I've never seen a bigger baby in my life than a man who's got a minor case of the flu. Most of them act as though we should call in the World Health Organization."

"I suppose you're going to drag the horrors of giving birth into this now—which, I'll remind you, is completely unfair."

"I don't need to. Men have a hard time just dealing with a simple cold. If God had left procreation up to the male of the species, humanity would've died out with Adam."

"That's three," Jason muttered ungraciously. "Three is not several. Three is a *few.*"

Charlotte shook her head. "It's enough. You don't have a leg to stand on, but you're too proud to admit it, which is something else a woman's more capable of doing."

"What? Standing on one leg?"

"No, admitting she's wrong. Don't get me started on that one. It happens to be a personal peeve of mine."

"You mean the others weren't?"

"Not particularly. I was just listing a few of the more obvious facts, waiting for you to come up with even one logical defense — which you failed to do."

He didn't seem willing to agree, but it was apparent from the smile he ineffectively struggled to hide that he was aware of his dilemma. He had no option, no argument.

"You realize you've backed me into a corner, don't you? I don't have any choice but to agree with you, otherwise you'll brand me as being smug and insensitive, unaware of my feelings and too childish to accept the truth."

"I suppose you're right." If anyone was wearing a smug look, it was Charlotte. She felt triumphant, better than she had all day. All week. Come to think of it, she couldn't remember when she'd enjoyed herself more.

Conceding defeat, Jason moved into the kitchen and returned with a second cold beer for each of them. Charlotte hesitated. She'd never intended to stay this long, and Carrie might be concerned. After all the lectures she'd delivered about being gone longer than expected, Charlotte felt she should go home now. But, to her amazement, she discovered she didn't want to leave. Watching the rest of the Lakers game with Jason appealed to her a lot more.

"Thanks, anyway, but I should get back to Carrie," she said.

Although she smiled brightly, some of her reluctance must have shown because Jason said, "So soon?"

"I stayed much longer than I'd planned to."

"But the game's only half over."

"I know, but..."

"Why don't you call her?" Jason suggested, pointing toward the counter where he kept his phone.

It seemed like a reasonable idea. Charlotte smiled and headed for the kitchen. She punched out her number and waited. Carrie answered on the third ring.

"Oh, hi, Mom," she said in an unconcerned voice.

"I'm watching the Lakers game with Jason."

"Okay. We're not going to move, are we?"

"No, Jason was kind enough to let me withdraw my two-weeks' notice."

"Oh, good. He's a great guy, isn't he?"

"Yeah." Charlotte was surprised by how much she meant it. Jason *was* a great guy. She hadn't stumbled on many in the past few—or was that several?—years. It was a treat to encounter a man who was candid, sincere and fun. But Charlotte had been fooled by men before, so she wasn't taking anything for granted.

"Well?" Jason asked when she replaced the receiver.

If she needed an excuse, he was handing her one on a platter. All she needed to do was make some vague reply about Carrie and she'd be on her way.

"Carrie says she'll call if she needs me."

"Excellent."

His smile was definitely charming, Charlotte decided.

"How about some popcorn?" he asked.

Charlotte nodded eagerly. She hadn't eaten much dinner, unnerved as she was by her discovery, knowing she'd need to confront him. Jason's offhand acceptance of her apology endeared him to her even more. If Jason was like her boss, he'd have flayed her alive. Instead, he'd just shrugged it off and given her a beer.

"Let me help," she said, following him into the kitchen.

"There's not much to do," he said, opening his microwave and tossing a bag inside. He set the timer, pushed a button and within a minute the sound of popping kernels filled the kitchen. The smell was heavenly.

When it was ready, Jason poured the popcorn into a large bowl and carried it out to the living room. Charlotte brought paper towels, since she couldn't find any napkins.

He placed the bowl in the middle of the coffee table and Charlotte joined him on the sofa. The game was about to resume. She tucked her feet beneath her as she'd done earlier, leaning forward now and then to scoop up some popcorn. It tasted wonderful, but that might've been because of the company. Or the fact that for the first time all day, she was feeling relaxed.

The Lakers scored twelve straight points and Charlotte rose to her knees, cheering loudly. Normally she was far more reserved, more in control of her emotions. It was as if someone else had taken charge of her mind. Someone more free-spirited and uninhibited. Someone who'd downed two beers on a near-empty stomach. Apparently, hearing that her daughter was bribing men to date her had that kind of effect on her.

Jason cheered, too, and they turned to smile at each other. Their eyes met and held for the longest time. Flustered and unnerved, Charlotte was the first to glance away.

She hadn't shared such an intense look with a man since college. A look that said, I'm enjoying myself. I'm attracted to you. I'd like to get to know you better…a whole lot better.

Her heart was thumping as she forced her attention back to the TV. She took a deep swallow of beer to hide her discomfort.

Jason went strangely quiet afterward, too. They both made a pretense of being involved in the game. As time went on, however, it wasn't the Lakers who held their attention— it was each other.

"So," Jason said abruptly, "where do you work?"

"Downtown, for a large insurance agency. You might've heard of them. Davidson and Krier. They have a radio commercial that's played a lot." In an effort, weak though it was, to disguise her uneasiness, she sang the all-too-familiar jingle.

"I have heard of them," Jason said, nodding. His rich baritone concluded the song.

They laughed self-consciously. Charlotte wished she'd had the sense to leave at half-time. No, she amended silently, that wasn't true. She was glad she'd stayed. If she regretted anything, it was that she was so clumsy when it came to dealing with male-female relationships.

Maybe it wasn't so strange that Carrie had tried to bribe someone to ask her on a date. Charlotte hadn't been out with a man in three years. But she hadn't really missed the dating scene. How could she miss something she'd never actually experienced? She'd hardly dated at all since Tom left.

Tom. The accustomed pain she felt whenever she thought of her ex-husband followed on the heels of the unexpected attraction she felt toward Jason. The two didn't mix well. One brought back the pain of the past and reminded her that she had no future. The other tempted her to believe she did.

"I should be going," she announced suddenly, her decision made. She scurried to her feet as if she had a pressing appointment.

"The game's not over," Jason said, frowning. He didn't move for a moment. "Don't go yet."

"I'll watch the rest of it at my place. Thanks

so much for the wonderful evening. I enjoyed myself. Really, I did." She picked up the empty popcorn bowl and the two beer bottles and took them into the kitchen.

Jason trailed her, his hands buried deep in his pockets. He nodded at his garbage can, which was overflowing. There was a semi-circle of half-filled bags stacked around it.

"I've been meaning to take this out to the Dumpster," he explained, removing the bottles from her hands and throwing them into a plastic recycling bin.

"I appreciate how understanding you've been," Charlotte said as she walked to the door.

"About what?" he asked.

"Carrie and me and…everything."

"No problem," he said a few steps behind. He slipped in front of her and stood by the door.

Charlotte knew she was running away like a frightened rabbit. The trapped feeling had returned and it terrified her as it always had. She'd thought it would be different this time, but that had been the beer. Her fears would never change, never go away. They'd always be there to remind her of her shortcomings, how inadequate she was, how no man could ever be trusted. Tom had proved that. She was anxious to be on her way now, but Jason was blocking her only means of escape.

When she glanced up, some of the fear must have shown in her eyes because he hesitated, studying her.

There was a short silence, too deep to last long, but too intense to ignore. Charlotte held his gaze for as long as she dared before looking away. His eyes were so blue, so serious, so filled with questions. She'd perplexed him, she knew, but she couldn't explain. *Wouldn't* explain.

They'd laughed and teased and joked. But Jason was somber now. Funny, this mood was as appealing as the lightheartedness she'd sensed in him earlier. His mouth, even when he wasn't smiling, was perfectly shaped. Everything about him was perfect. His high cheekbones, his wide brow and straight nose. Too perfect for her.

The paralyzing regret threatened to explode within her, but Charlotte managed to keep it in check. How, she wasn't sure. It must've been her fear, she decided. Fear of what could happen, the happiness a relationship with him could bring—and the disappointment that would inevitably come afterward. The disappointment he'd feel in her. Then it would be over almost before it had begun.

She looked up one last time, to say goodbye, to thank him, to escape.

In that instant she knew Jason was going to kiss her. But one word, the least bit of resistance, and he wouldn't go through with it. Charlotte was completely confident of that.

Need and curiosity overcame the anxiety, and she watched, mesmerized, as his mouth descended toward her own. His lips, so warm and seductive, barely touched hers.

Charlotte closed her eyes, trembling and afraid. Her body, seemingly of its own accord, moved toward him, turning into his, seeking the security and the strength she felt in him.

He moaned softly and Charlotte did, too, slanting her head to one side, inviting him to deepen the kiss.

Yet Jason held back. The kiss was light. Sweet. More seductive than anything she'd ever known. It felt wonderful. So wonderful...

Charlotte didn't understand why he resisted kissing her completely, the way her body was begging him to. Restraining himself demanded obvious effort. She could tell by the rigid way he held himself, the way his hands curved over her shoulders, keeping her at bay. Keeping himself at bay.

Her head was full of the promise his lips had made and hadn't kept. Full of the possibilities. Full of the surprise and the wonder. She'd never felt like this before.

Once again his mouth brushed over hers, warm and exciting. Moving slowly—so slowly—and so easy, as though he had all the time in the world.

"Jason." It was a battle for her to breathe. Her heart sounded like a frantic drumbeat in her ears, drowning out coherent thought.

He tensed, then kissed her, really kissed her, wrapping himself around her, absorbing her in his size, his strength, his need.

They remained entwined, arms around each other, until Charlotte could no longer stand. She broke away and buried her head in his shoulder, her breathing heavy.

"Charlotte, I didn't mean to frighten you."

"You didn't." It was the truth; any fear she felt had nothing to do with him. "I have to go… Thank you. For everything."

But most of all for that kiss, she added silently. It was unlikely he'd ever know how much that single kiss had meant to her.

Three

He'd kissed her. He'd actually kissed Charlotte. An hour later, Jason still had trouble taking it in.

Oh, he'd kissed plenty of women in his day. But this time, with this woman, it was different. He didn't know how he understood that, but he did. He'd realized it long before he'd touched her. Perhaps because she was so different from what he'd assumed. He'd figured she was dignified, straitlaced, unapproachable. Then, as soon as he'd told her about basketball rules, she'd kicked off her shoes and was cheering as enthusiastically as he was himself. What a contrast he found in her. Prim and proper on the outside, a hellion waiting to break loose on the inside.

She intrigued him. Beguiled him.

At some point during their evening together—exactly when, he couldn't be sure— he'd felt an unfamiliar tug, a stirring deep within. The feeling hadn't gone away. If anything, it had intensified.

What they'd shared wasn't any ordinary kiss, either. Perhaps that explained it. They'd communicated on an entirely different level, one he'd never known before. It seemed their spirits—the deepest, innermost part of themselves—had somehow touched. He shook his head. He was getting fanciful.

No, this wasn't the kind of kiss he'd had with any other woman. He'd never gone so slowly, been so careful. Although she'd acted blatantly provocative, urging him to deepen the contact, he'd resisted. That same inner voice that had said Charlotte was different had also warned him to proceed with caution. He'd sensed how fragile she was, and the urge to protect her, even from himself, had been overwhelming.

Jason wasn't generally so philosophical. He didn't waste time deliberating on relationships or motivations. He wasn't sure what he was thinking right now. His reaction to Charlotte was unwarranted—wasn't it? Although it'd been a nice kiss, it wasn't so spectacular

that his whole world should be turned upside down.

Yet it was—flipped over completely.

Jason felt almost giddy with sensation.
These feelings weren't logical. It was as if
God had decided to play a world-class trick
on him.

Jason considered himself too old for romance. He didn't even know what romance
was. Pure foolishness, he thought sarcastically. It was one of the primary reasons he'd
never married, and never intended to. He
wasn't a romantic kind of guy. A pizza and
cold beer while watching a football game interested him far more than staring across a
candlelit table at some woman and pretending to be overwhelmed by her beauty. Flat-
tery and small talk weren't for him.

And yet…he remembered how good Charlotte's arms had felt around his neck. She'd
held her body so tightly against his that he
could feel her heart beat. It was a closeness
that had transcended the physical.

By the time she'd left, Jason felt heady, as if
he'd had too much to drink. He didn't understand her rush, either. He hadn't wanted her
to leave and had tried to come up with a rea-

son for her to stay. Any reason. But she'd quietly slipped out of his arms and left before he could think of a way to keep her there. If he was witty and romantic he might've thought of something. But he wasn't, so he'd been forced to let her go.

Jason started pacing, the Lakers game forgotten. He needed to clear the cobwebs from his head. He wasn't any good at analyzing situations like this. All he knew was that he'd enjoyed holding Charlotte in his arms, enjoyed kissing her, and he looked forward to doing it again.

He sank down in front of the television, surprised to find the basketball game already over. Stunned, he stared at the credits rolling down the screen. He didn't even know who won. He waited, hoping the camera would scan the scoreboard, but it didn't happen.

He had a bet riding on the outcome of the game. Nothing major, just a friendly wager between brothers. Nevertheless, high stakes or low, it wasn't like Jason Manning to be caught without a final score.

The phone rang and Jason hurried to the kitchen to answer it.

"Hello," he said absently, keeping his eye

on the television, still hoping to learn the final outcome.

"I knew I never should've picked the Nuggets," Rich muttered.

"You mean the Lakers won?"

"By eight points. Where have *you* been all evening?"

"Home," Jason returned defensively. "I had company. A tenant stopped in to chat."

"During a play-off game, and you didn't get rid of them?"

Actually Jason hadn't intended to tell his brother even that much, but Rich had a point. Jason wasn't one to sit around and shoot the breeze when he could be watching a game. Any kind of game.

"It was business," he explained, unnecessarily annoyed. He felt mildly guilty for stretching the truth. Charlotte's original intent had been to apologize and tell him she'd changed her mind about moving. That was business. Staying the better part of two hours wasn't.

Ignoring Jason's bad mood, Rich chatted on, replaying the last half of the fourth quarter in which the Lakers had made an "amazing" comeback. While his brother was speaking, Jason glanced at the list of his tenants' phone numbers, which he kept by the phone for easy reference. The way his eyes immediately latched on to Charlotte's name, anyone might think it had been circled in red. He was so distracted by reading her name over and over in his mind that he missed most of what Rich was telling him.

When the conversation with his brother ended, Jason couldn't recall more than a few words of what they'd said. Just enough to regret that he hadn't been watching the game. Just enough to wish he'd thought of something that would've prompted Charlotte to stay.

Without a second's deliberation, he reached for his phone and dialed her number. Carrie answered before the first ring had been completed. She must not have recognized his voice, because she got Charlotte without comment.

"Hello."

"Hi," he said, feeling gauche. "The Lakers won."

"I know."

Apparently their kiss hadn't deranged her the way it had him. She must have gone back to her apartment, plunked herself down and watched the rest of the game, while he'd been walking around in a stupor for the past hour.

"I was thinking," Jason began, "about dinner tomorrow night. That is, if you're free."

"Dinner," she repeated as if this was a foreign concept. "What time?" she asked a moment later.

"Six."

"Sure."

His mood lightened. "Great, I'll pick you up then." He replaced the receiver and glanced around his kitchen, frustrated by how messy it was. He hated housework, hated having to pick up after himself, hated the everyday chores that made life so mundane. Every dish he owned was dirty, except the ones in his dishwasher, which were clean. It didn't make sense to reload it while there were clean dishes he could use in there.

Needing something to occupy his mind, he tackled the task of cleaning up the kitchen with unprecedented enthusiasm.

Jason's eagerness to see Charlotte again had waned by the following afternoon. A good night's sleep and a day at the clinic had sufficiently straightened out his brain. He'd behaved in a manner that was completely out of character. He couldn't even begin to figure out why.

Charlotte was a woman. There wasn't anything special about her. No reason he should be falling all over himself for the opportunity to take her out. He'd missed the last half of an important basketball game because his thoughts had become so tangled up with her. That would've been devotion enough for any woman in his life—only she wasn't in his life, and he intended to keep it that way.

Furthermore, Jason wasn't that keen on Charlotte's teenage daughter thinking he'd fallen in with her scheme. He could see it now. Carrie would give him a brilliant smile and a high-five when he arrived. The girl was bound to believe she was responsible for Jason asking Charlotte out. She might even try to slip him some of the money she'd offered him earlier. The whole thing had the potential for disaster written all over it.

If a convenient excuse to cancel this date had presented itself, Jason would've grabbed it with both hands.

The way his luck was going, they'd probably run into his parents, and his mother would start hounding him again about getting married. He'd never understood why women considered marriage so important. Frustrated, he'd asked his mother once, and her answer had confused him even more. She'd looked at him serenely without interrupting the task that occupied her hands and had casually said, "It's good to have a partner."

A partner! She'd made it sound like he needed a wife in order to compete in a mixed bowling league.

His parents weren't exactly throwing potential mates his way, but they'd let it be known that they were hoping he'd get married sometime soon. Jason, however, was intelligent enough not to become involved in a lifetime relationship just to satisfy his parents' wishes.

Whatever craziness had prompted him to ask Charlotte out to dinner had passed during the night. He'd awakened sane and in command of his usual common sense.

As the day went on he found himself actually dreading the date. The two of them had absolutely nothing in common. He'd go through with this, Jason decided grimly, because he was a man of his word. Since he told her he'd be there by six, he would be, but snow would fall at the equator before he gave in to an impulse like this again.

* * *

She was dressed completely wrong, Charlotte realized as soon as Jason arrived. Not knowing what to wear, she'd chosen a navy blue suit, not unlike the one she'd worn to the office. She'd attempted to dress it up a bit with a bright turquoise-and-pink scarf and a quarter-size silver pin of a colorful toucan. Jason arrived in jeans, sweatshirt and a baseball cap with a University of Washington Huskies logo on it.

"Hello," she said, forcing herself to smile. A hundred times in the last hour she'd regretted ever agreeing to this date. Jason had caught her off guard when he'd phoned. She hadn't known what to say. Hadn't had time to think of an excuse.

Now she was stuck, but judging by his expression, Jason didn't seem any more pleased than she was. He frowned at her until she was so self-conscious, she suggested changing clothes.

"Don't worry about it," he muttered, tucking the tips of his fingers into his back pockets. They definitely made a pair. He'd dressed like someone visiting the amusement park, and she looked like a student of Emily Post.

Charlotte was grateful that Carrie had gone

to the library with a friend. The other mom was picking them up, but it would give Charlotte a convenient excuse to hurry home.

"Where would you like to eat?" Jason asked once they were outside the apartment.

"Wherever you want."

"Mexican food?" He didn't sound enthusiastic.

"Fine." Especially since there was a restaurant close by. "How about Mr. Tamales on Old Military Road?"

"Sure," he agreed easily enough. He was probably thinking the same thing she was. The sooner they got there, the sooner they'd be finished and could go back to their respective lives instead of dabbling in this nonsense.

For the short time they were together, Charlotte figured she might as well enjoy herself. The restaurant was little more than a greasy spoon, but the food had earned its excellent reputation.

The place apparently did a brisk business on weeknights because there was only one spot available.

"I never would've thought we'd need reservations," Jason said, looking as surprised as Charlotte.

The hostess, wearing an off-the-shoulder peasant blouse and black skirt, smiled and escorted them to the booth. The waitress followed close behind. She handed them each a menu shaped like a cactus and then brought water, tortilla chips and salsa. Charlotte read over the choices, made her selection and scooped up a jalapeño pepper with a chip.

"You aren't going to eat that, are you?" Jason asked, staring at her as if she'd pulled the pin activating a grenade.

Charlotte grinned. "Oh, that's another thing I forgot to mention last night—women can eat chili peppers better than a man."

"Not this time, sweetheart. I was weaned on hot peppers." He took one, poising it in front of his mouth.

"Me, too," she challenged.

They bit into the peppers simultaneously. The seeds and juice dribbled down Charlotte's chin and she grabbed a paper napkin, dabbing it against her skin.

"You weren't kidding," Jason said, obviously impressed.

"I never kid." A five-alarm fire was blazing in her mouth, but she smiled and reached casually for another chip and some water. The water intensified the burning, but she smiled cheerfully as though nothing was wrong.

"Rich and I used to eat these peppers right out of Dad's garden."

"I take it Rich is your brother?"

"I'm one of five," Jason went on to explain, and she noted that his eyes brightened with pride. "Paul's the oldest, then there's me, followed by Rich. My sisters, Taylor and Christy, round out the family."

"Are any of them married?"

"Everyone but me. I'm beginning to lose track of how many nieces and nephews I've got now, and there doesn't seem to be a lull yet."

Charlotte had never had much of a family. Her father had deserted her and her mother when Charlotte was too young to remember him. Then her mother had died just about the time Charlotte graduated from high school. The insurance money was set up to cover her college expenses. Only the money hadn't been used for her. Instead, Tom had been educated on her inheritance; he'd robbed her of even that.

Charlotte lowered her gaze. It hurt too much to think about Tom and that bleak period of her life when she'd been so lost and vulnerable. So alone, with no family. Her ex-husband had used her and when he'd finished, he'd thrown her aside.

All the time she was growing up, Charlotte had dreamed about being part of a large, loving family. How she envied Jason his brothers and sisters.

"The story of my family tree is less about the roots," he said, grinning as he spoke, "than the sap."

Charlotte's laugh was spontaneous. She picked up her water, warmed by his wit and his willingness to laugh at himself. "I was an only child. I promised myself I'd have a houseful of kids when I got married so my children wouldn't grow up lonely."

"Lonely," Jason echoed. "I would have given anything for some peace and quiet. The girls were the worst."

"Somehow I guessed you'd complain about the women in your family."

"You know," he said, "I never thought I'd say this, but I really miss Taylor and Christy. They're both living in Montana now, raising their families. We get together when we can, which isn't nearly often enough. It's been over a year since we saw each other."

The waitress came for their order. Charlotte asked for the specialty salad, which consisted of beans, rice, cheese, shredded chicken, lettuce and slices of tomato and jalapeño peppers. Jason chose the chicken enchiladas.

"Do your brothers live in the Seattle area?"

Jason nodded. "Paul's a journalist and Rich works as an engineer for Boeing. We see each other frequently."

Their orders arrived and they chatted amicably over their meal. Jason sampled her salad and fed her a bite of his enchiladas; both were delicious. Soon they'd asked the waitress for two additional plates and were unabashedly sharing their meals.

It was only seven-thirty when they'd finished, even though they lingered over coffee. Charlotte couldn't remember time passing more quickly.

All day she'd been worried about this dinner—and for nothing. She'd enjoyed herself even more than she'd hoped, but that was easy to do with Jason. He didn't put on airs or pretend to be something he wasn't. Nor did he feign agreement with her; their differing opinions meant a free and interesting exchange of ideas.

"I should be heading home," Charlotte said, although she could happily have sat there talking. They weren't at a loss for topics, but the restaurant was busy and Carrie would be home soon.

"Yeah, I suppose we should go," he said reluctantly, standing. He left a generous tip and took the tab up to the counter.

After talking nonstop for nearly an hour, both were strangely quiet on the drive home. Charlotte had been determined to enjoy herself from the start, but she'd expected to make the best of a bad situation. Instead she'd had a wonderful time.

She hadn't known how starved she was for adult companionship, hadn't realized how empty she'd felt inside, how deep the void had become.

As they neared the apartment complex, she realized one more thing. She didn't want this evening to end.

"Would you like to come in for coffee?" she asked as he parked his car. For half the ride home, Charlotte had been engaging in a silent debate. She was sure that if Carrie was home, she'd make a big deal about Jason's presence. But Charlotte would get the third degree from her daughter anyway, so she decided it didn't matter if Jason came in.

"I could use another cup of coffee," Jason

told her, although they'd both had large mugs at the restaurant.

As luck would have it, Carrie wasn't home yet. Charlotte had been counting on her teenage daughter to act as a buffer between her and Jason. She half suspected Jason was thinking the same thing.

"Carrie's at the library with a friend," she explained. "But I'm sure she'll be back any minute."

"I wondered what she was up to tonight."

"I'll put on the coffee," she said self-consciously, going directly to the kitchen. "Make yourself at home."

While she scooped up the grounds and poured water into the pot, she saw that Jason had lowered himself onto her sofa. He reached for a magazine and flipped through the pages, then set it back and reached for another. Since it was upside down, his attention was clearly elsewhere. He noted his mistake, righted the magazine, then placed it with the others. Apparently *Seventeen* magazine didn't interest him after all.

There was no reason for him to be so nervous. It was funny; they'd chatted like old friends at the restaurant, but the instant they were alone, they became uncomfortable with each other.

"I thought you might like some cookies," she said, as she carried the tray into the living room. She'd baked chocolate chip cookies that weekend, and there were plenty left over.

Being a single mother left her vulnerable to attacks of guilt—guilt that often led to an abundance of homemade cookies. There were so many things she didn't know about family, so much she'd missed out on. It bothered her more than she wanted to admit. Whenever Charlotte was feeling anxious or contrite about something, she baked. And with the ninth-grade dance hanging over her head, she'd been doing a lot of baking lately. The cookie jar was full. The freezer was packed, too. Even Carrie was complaining about all the goodies around the house. Too tempting, she said. Her daughter claimed Charlotte was trying to raise her cholesterol and kill her off.

More guilt, more need to bake cookies. It was a vicious circle.

"Homemade cookies," Jason said, sliding forward, far more appreciative than her daughter. "I didn't know anyone but my mother baked these days." He took one and downed it in two bites, nodding vigorously even before he'd finished chewing.

Charlotte smiled at the unspoken compliment and poured their coffee in plain white china cups. "There's plenty more where those came from."

Jason helped himself to a second and then a third.

Charlotte was pleased that he seemed to value her culinary skills. "I guess it's true, then."

He cocked one eyebrow. "What?"

"Never mind," she muttered, sorry she'd brought up the subject.

"If you're thinking the way to a man's heart is through his stomach, forget it. Others before you have tried that route."

"Several dozen, no doubt," she teased, amused by his complete lack of modesty. Not to mention his arrogance.

"I've suffered my share of feminine wiles."

"Feminine wiles," Charlotte repeated, trying hard not to laugh out loud. He acted as though she was setting a trap for him. She was about to reassure him that she had no intention of remarrying, then decided against it. She'd let him assume whatever he wanted.

After all, he was helping her get rid of these cookies before they overran the apartment.

She did bring up another topic, though, one she couldn't help being curious about. "Why aren't you married?" She hoped he wouldn't be offended by her directness; based on their previous conversations she didn't expect him to be.

Jason shrugged and swallowed the last bite of the last cookie she'd set out. He seemed to be thinking over his response as he picked up his coffee and relaxed against the back of the sofa. "I learned something recently about the differences between a man and a woman. It's information that's served me well."

They certainly had a routine going with this subject. "Oh, what's that?"

"Tell me, all kidding aside," he said, his blue eyes serious, "what is it women want from a man?"

Charlotte thought about that for a moment. "To be loved."

He nodded approvingly.

"To be needed and respected."

"Exactly." He grinned, clearly pleased by her answer.

He was making this easy, and Charlotte warmed to her ideas. "A woman longs to be held, of course, but more than that, she wants to be treasured, appreciated."

"Perfect," Jason said, smiling benignly. "Now ask me what a man wants."

"All right," she said, crossing her legs, holding the saucer with one hand, her cup in the other. "What is it a man wants?"

"Tickets to the World Series," Jason returned without a pause.

Charlotte nearly choked on her laughter. Fortunately she wasn't swallowing a sip of coffee at the time. "I see what you mean," she said after she'd composed herself. "There does seem to be a basic, shall we say, disconnect here."

He nodded. "It was when Rich gave up two tickets for a Seahawks football game that I knew he'd fallen in love."

"That's sweet," Charlotte said with a sigh, enjoying the romance of it all.

"Don't go all soft on me. It wasn't like it sounds. He gave the tickets to a friend as a bribe. Rich didn't want to date Jamie himself, he wanted someone else to fall in love with her."

"He bribed another guy to take her out?"

"Yup. He was in love with her himself, but like the rest of us, he's useless when it comes to romance. I figured it out before he did, and I know next to nothing about that kind of stuff." Jason grinned. "From that point on, it was all downhill for Rich. He's married and has a couple of kids now. A girl and a boy."

"I don't care what you say. That's sweet."

"Perhaps."

Charlotte was relaxed now. She removed her shoes and propped her feet on the coffee table, crossing her legs at the ankles. "Have *you* ever been in love?" At Jason's hesitation, she hurried to add, "I shouldn't have asked that."

"I don't mind, if you won't take offense at my answer—which is, I don't know. I thought I was once, several years back, but in retrospect I'm not sure. It hurt when we broke up, and I was sorry we hadn't been able to work things out, but I don't have any real regrets."

"What was her name?"

"Julie. She's married now."

Charlotte didn't understand where she found the courage, but she reached forward and brushed her index finger down the side of Jason's face. She wanted to ease the pain she read in his expression, the pain he discounted so casually. A pain she recognized, since she'd walked through this valley herself, with the cold wind of despair howling at her back.

Jason's gaze met hers and she felt immersed in a look so warm, so intense, that her breath caught. She couldn't remember a man ever looking at her that way, as though he wasn't sure she was even real. As if he was afraid she'd vanish if he touched her.

Jason removed the cup and saucer from her hands and set them on the tray next to the empty plate.

He was going to kiss her; she realized it in the same moment she owned up to how much she wanted him to. All night she'd been looking forward to having him do exactly this, only she hadn't been willing to admit it.

His mouth was gentle and sweet with the taste of coffee and chocolate. He kissed her the way he had the night before, and Charlotte could barely take in the sensation that overwhelmed her. She'd never thought she'd feel anything so profound, so exciting, again. She hadn't believed she was capable of such a rush of feeling....

She whimpered and wrapped her arms around his neck, holding on to him in a world that had started to spin out of control. His hands framed her face and he slanted his mouth over hers, answering her need with his own.

Jason kissed her again and again.

The sound coming from the front door barely registered in her passion-drugged brain.

"Mom...Jason..." was followed by a shocked pause, then, "Wow, this is great."

Charlotte broke away from Jason and leapt to her feet.

"Gee, Mom, there's no need to get embarrassed. People kiss all the time." Carrie floated across the carpet, then threw herself into a chair. "So," she said, smiling broadly, "is there anything either of you want to tell me?"

"Like what?" Charlotte asked.

Carrie shrugged with utter nonchalance. "That you're getting married?"

Four

On his way back to his apartment, Jason had to admit that Charlotte's daughter possessed a knack for the unexpected. Arriving when she did was only the beginning; introducing the subject of marriage had nearly sent him into hysterics.

Him married? It was downright laughable.

Thinking about it, Jason realized Charlotte had brought up the subject herself, wanting to know why he hadn't married, asking him if he'd ever been in love. Typical women questions.

Perhaps mother and daughter were in cahoots, plotting his downfall. No, that was equally laughable.

Jason simply wasn't the marrying kind. Not because he was a womanizer or because he had anything against the opposite sex. He liked women…at times and enjoyed being with them…occasionally. Liked kissing them… definitely. But he relished his freedom too much to sacrifice it to commitment and responsibility.

No, he told himself resolutely, Charlotte wasn't involved in any scheme to drag him to the altar. She'd been so embarrassed and flustered by Carrie's suggestion, her face had gone bright red. The woman's face was too open to hide her feelings. She had chastised Carrie, asked for and received an apology, and looked genuinely grateful when Jason said it was time he left.

Despite the episode with Carrie, Jason had thoroughly enjoyed his evening with Charlotte. He hadn't expected to. In fact he'd originally regretted having asked her out, but in the end their date had been a pleasant success.

Once again he was bewildered by the strong desire he experienced when he kissed her. He had ordained a hands-off policy for the night, but had shelved that idea the minute she'd sat next to him, gazing up at him with those pretty eyes of hers.

Actually, he'd known he was in trouble when he accepted her invitation to come inside for coffee. He'd thought of it as a challenge; he'd wanted to see how far he could push his determination. Not far, he concluded. When she'd looked at him, her eyes soft and inviting, he was lost. His hands-off policy had quickly become a hands-on experiment.

There was something about Charlotte Weston that got to him. Really got to him.

All that outward confidence she worked so hard to display hadn't fooled him. Beneath a paper-thin veneer, she was vulnerable. Any fool with two functional brain cells would have figured that out on the first date.

Only she didn't date.

Carrie had told him it'd been years since her mother had even gone out with a man. Undoubtedly she'd been asked—and if she hadn't been, why not? She was attractive, intelligent and fun. Offhand, he knew a half-dozen men who'd jump at the chance to meet a woman like Charlotte.

If she'd turned down offers, and surely she had, then there must be a reason. The question that confused Jason was: If she didn't date, then why had she agreed to have dinner with him?

Probably the same reason that had goaded him to ask, Jason concluded. The kiss. That infamous first kiss. It had rocked them both.

Taken them by surprise, leaving them excited—and unsure.

As for the other questions that hounded him, Jason didn't have any answers. Nor did he understand everything that was happening between him and Charlotte. One thing he did know—and it terrified him the most— was that they were, in effect, playing with lighted sticks of dynamite, tossing them back and forth. The attraction between them was that explosive. That dangerous.

Carrie's arrival had been more timely than she'd realized.

All right, Jason was willing to own up, albeit grudgingly, that he was fascinated with Charlotte. He suspected she'd confess to feeling the same thing. To his way of thinking, if they were so strongly attracted to each other, they should both be prepared to do something about it.

In other words, they should stop fighting the inevitable and make love. That would get it out of their system—he hoped.

Naw, Jason mused darkly. Charlotte wasn't the kind of woman who'd indulge in an affair. She might wear only straight, dark business suits to work, but deep down she was the romantic type, which made her impractical.

Most women seemed to be. If they were going to make love, they wanted it prettied up with a bunch of flowery words, a declaration of undying love and promises of commitment.

Well, Charlotte, along with every other woman, could forget that, he told himself. As far as he was concerned, romance and commitment were out of the question.

What he wanted in this relationship was honesty. If it were up to him, he'd suggest they do away with the formalities, admit what they wanted and then scratch that itch.

He mulled that over for a few minutes, knowing it was unlikely that Charlotte would see the situation his way. He might not know her well, but Jason readily acknowledged that she wasn't going to be satisfied with so little. Women tended to see lovemaking as more than just the relief of a physical craving.

Well, he, for one, wasn't going to play that game. He liked Charlotte—how much he liked her surprised him—but he knew the rules. Either they dropped everything now, while they still could, or they continued driving each other insane. Sooner or later, one of them would have to give in.

Without a second's hesitation, Jason knew it would be him.

Charlotte affected him deep down. He couldn't bear the thought of hurting her or causing her one second of unhappiness. In the end he'd say all the words she wanted to hear, and he'd do the best job he could, because pleasing her would mean so much to him.

Then he'd get what he wanted; she'd make love to him willingly, with everything in her. He'd give her all he had, too. The problem was—and he knew it was inevitable—that before he'd quite figured out what was happening, they'd be talking about marriage, which was something he hadn't done since Julie.

Jason stopped right there. If he started thinking along those lines, everything would change. Soon Charlotte would be organizing his life, straightening up his apartment, making suggestions about little things he could do to improve his sorry lot. Women always saw his lot as sorry. He was happy living the way he was, but women couldn't accept that. They didn't believe a man could survive without them constantly fussing over him, dictating his life.

Bit by bit, Charlotte would dominate his world, eroding his independence until he was like every other married man he'd ever known—willing to change his ways for a wife. Picking up his socks, getting hassled about sports games on TV, the whole deal.

No, the domesticated life wasn't for him. Still, Charlotte tempted him more than anyone else had in ages, and he could *almost* imagine their lives together. Not quite, but almost.

He stared at his apartment door, wondering how long he'd been standing there mulling over his thoughts. He was light-years ahead of himself, he realized. Good grief, he was already trying to finagle his way out of marrying her and they'd only gone out on one date. He'd only kissed her twice.

But, oh, those kisses...

Like he'd told himself before, they were playing with explosives, and the best way to avoid getting hurt was to get out now, before they became too involved. Before he lost the strength to walk away from her.

"Aren't you going to *do* something?" Carrie demanded.

"About what?" Charlotte returned calmly, feigning ignorance. She glanced up from her novel, looking over the rims of her reading glasses with practiced innocence.

"Jason!" Carrie cried. "You haven't heard from him in a whole week."

"Has it been that long?" Seven days, two hours and three minutes, but who was counting? Certainly not her.

"Mom," Carrie insisted, hands on her hips, "you know how long it's been. You jump every time the phone rings. You keep making excuses about checking the mail and getting the newspaper. We both know you're hoping to run into Jason."

It hurt Charlotte's pride to learn she'd been so obvious.

"You like him, don't you?" Carrie asked. Her expression said that if *she* were in charge, this romance would be making far greater progress. Charlotte, however, had no intention of letting her daughter take control of her relationship with Jason Manning.

"I think Jason's wonderful," Charlotte admitted softly. She did like her landlord. Yet, at the same time, she was grateful he hadn't taken the initiative and contacted her again. If he had, she wasn't sure how she would've responded.

"If you're so crazy about him, then do something about it," Carrie said again.

"Like what?" Even if Charlotte had a drawerful of ideas, she doubted she'd ever find the courage to use any of them. She didn't know how to chase after a man and had no interest in doing so.

"You're asking me?" Carrie asked. "C'mon, who's the kid here?" She launched herself onto the cushion beside Charlotte. "What went wrong?" she asked, looking up at her mother with mournful eyes. "The two of you seemed to be getting along really well when I walked in last week."

Charlotte slid her arm around Carrie's shoulders. Despite her efforts not to, she grinned, remembering when she, too, had been so wise and confident.

"It might've had something to do with the subject of marriage—which *you* brought up. He seemed to get a bit green around the gills at that point."

"You think it frightened him off?" Carrie asked anxiously.

Charlotte shrugged. She'd brought up the subject herself, not quite as directly, but she *had* mentioned it. If ever there was a born bachelor, she decided, it was Jason Manning. Together, mother and daughter had managed to terrify the man. He must think they were sitting in their apartment ready to ambush him, tie him up and drag him in front of the closest preacher.

Charlotte wasn't sure what she wanted anymore. Perhaps she was protecting her ego by convincing herself that she wouldn't have gone out with Jason if he'd asked again. Perhaps it was just her pride. Charlotte didn't know because the opportunity hadn't come up.

She was embarrassed to admit it, but what Carrie had said about her hanging around the mailbox hoping to *accidentally* run into Jason was true. But she wasn't looking for a way to get him to ask her out, she told herself. She only wanted to set things straight. Since they hadn't met, accidentally or otherwise, Charlotte was content to let it drop. He apparently was, too.

Jason Manning had been a brief but pleasant interlude in her—she had to acknowledge it—humdrum life.

She was grateful for their time together. He'd taught her everything she needed to know about basketball. He'd challenged her in a battle of wits about male and female roles in society. Convinced her never again to eat a jalapeño pepper to prove a point. And most important, he'd kissed her in a way that made her believe, for those few minutes, that she was whole and desirable. It'd felt so good to surrender her fears and her doubts. If nothing else, she'd always be grateful for that.

"Maybe he's waiting to hear from you," Carrie said next. "It's your turn to ask him out, isn't it?"

"It doesn't work that way with adults, sweetie." Although Charlotte had no idea if that was even true.

"Then it should. I'm not going to sit home and wait for a man to call me. If I like him, I'll phone him. It's ridiculous to be a slave to such an outdated tradition."

Charlotte agreed with her daughter, but in this instance she planned to do nothing at all. And that included hovering around the mailboxes.

It had been a long day, and Jason was tired when he pulled into the parking lot outside his apartment complex. He scanned the limited spaces, looking for Charlotte's car. The blue PT Cruiser was in the appropriate slot, so he knew she was home.

It wasn't that he was trying to run into her, but he wouldn't mind seeing her, finding out how she was doing—that sort of thing. He didn't intend anything more than a wave and maybe a friendly "I'm-fine-how-are-you?" exchange. Then he'd go about his business and she could go about hers.

Not calling Charlotte was proving to be more difficult than he'd ever expected. He thought about her even more now. He dreamed about her. Just that morning, the alarm had gone off and he was lying there in bed, trying to force himself to get up, when Charlotte casually sauntered into his mind. He couldn't help thinking how good it would feel to have her there beside him, how soft her body would feel next to his. He'd banished the thought immediately, angry about indulging in such a fantasy.

It had started the night before. When he'd arrived home from work, he'd found himself checking out the rear tire of Charlotte's car. From a distance it looked like it might be low on air. On closer examination, he realized it wasn't. He felt almost disappointed not to have an excuse to speak to her.

This evening he could tell from a distance that there wasn't anything wrong with her tires. Once again he wished there was, so he could talk to her.

Inside his apartment, he reached for the remote control and automatically turned on the television. The six-thirty news crew made for excellent company.

As the forecaster gave dire warnings about the weather, Jason checked out the meager contents of his refrigerator. One of these days he'd have to break down and buy groceries.

As he suspected, nothing interesting presented itself, at least nothing he'd seriously consider eating. An empty cardboard carton from a six-pack of beer. A can of half-eaten pork and beans. A leftover taco, probably harder than cement, wrapped in a napkin, and a jar of green olives. He opened the jar, stuck his hand inside and fished out the last two, returning the container of liquid to the shelf. Chewing on the olives, he closed the door.

What he was really in the mood for was— he hated to admit it. What he'd really like was chocolate chip cookies. Well, he could forget that. The store-bought ones tasted like lumpy paste, and his mother would keep him on the phone with an endless list of questions if he were to call her and request a batch. Besides, it wasn't his mother's recipe he craved. It was Charlotte's.

Well, you can forget that, ol' boy.

A box of macaroni and cheese was the

most interesting prospect his cupboard had to offer. He took it out and checked the freezer compartment of the refrigerator and brought out two frozen wieners wrapped in aluminum foil.

He was adding water to a pan when there was a frantic knocking on his door. Whoever it was pounded again before he had time to cross the apartment.

He saw Charlotte, pale and stricken, her lavender cardigan covered in blood. Her eyes were panicky. "A dog…someone ran over a dog…they didn't even stop. Please…can you come?"

"Of course." He kept a black bag at the house for just such emergencies. He grabbed that and hurried after her.

Charlotte was waiting for him, her eyes bright with tears. "He's unconscious."

"You moved him?"

"Only to get him out of the street."

"Did you see it happen?" he asked, trotting along behind her.

"No. I heard tires screech and a yelp, and that was it. By the time I got outside, a few kids had gathered around, but no one knew what to do."

Her pace slowed as they approached the injured animal. A group of neighborhood children had gathered around. Jason knelt beside the small, black dog. He was a mixed breed, mostly spaniel, Jason guessed. He was badly hurt and in shock. Probably a stray, since he wasn't wearing a collar, and the poor thing looked mangy and thin.

"Does anyone know who he belongs to?" Jason asked.

"I don't think he belongs to anyone," a boy on a bicycle answered. "He's been around the last couple of days. I never saw him before that."

"I'm going to take him to my office," Jason said after a preliminary examination. He didn't feel too positive about the dog's chances.

"Is he going to live?" Charlotte alone voiced the question, but she seemed to be the spokesperson for the small gathering— each one wanted, indeed needed, to know. The children and Charlotte stared down at Jason, waiting for his response.

"I'm not sure," Jason answered honestly. "He's got a broken leg and internal injuries."

"I'll pay for his medical expenses," Charlotte offered, using her index finger to wipe a tear from her eye.

Jason wasn't even thinking about the expenses. Frankly, he didn't think the dog would last the night. "Give me your sweater," he told Charlotte. Since it was already stained with blood, he figured they'd save time by using it to transport the injured dog.

She did as he asked, and he spread it out on the pavement, then placed the wounded dog on it. Jason carefully lifted him, using the sweater sleeves, and walked toward his car.

"I'll go with you," Charlotte said, while Jason placed the now-unconscious dog in the backseat.

"You're sure?" he asked. "This could take some time."

"I'm sure." Carrie came running up to the car. The girl had tears in her eyes, too. Mother and daughter briefly hugged before Carrie stepped away. She looked so mournful it was all Jason could do not to stop and reassure her. But he had no reassurances to offer.

His veterinary clinic was only a few blocks from the apartment complex. Charlotte followed him in. He set the injured dog on the stainless-steel examination table and turned on the lights above it. Charlotte's sweater was soaked with blood beyond the point of salvaging it, but she didn't seem concerned.

Jason examined the dog's injuries and it was as he'd feared: surgery would be required.

He told Charlotte and she nodded bravely. "Can I do anything? I'm not a nurse, but I'd like to assist—that is, if you think I'd be any help?"

Jason hesitated, uncertain, then decided. "You can if you really want to."

She nodded. "Please."

"You don't have to," he said. This wasn't going to be pretty and if she was the least bit squeamish, it would be better to sit out in the waiting room. He told her as much.

"I want to," she said confidently. "I can handle it."

Jason didn't take long to set up everything he needed for the surgery. They both scrubbed down and he gave her a green surgical cap and gown. He smiled at her before administering the anesthesia, taking pains to explain what he was doing and why.

The procedure didn't last more than an hour. When he'd finished, he transferred the dog to the hospital portion of his facility. There was a night-time staff member who'd watch over the spaniel and the other pets who required continuous care.

"What do you think?" she asked hopefully when he returned.

"It doesn't look promising," Jason told her. He didn't want to give her any false hopes or mislead her. "But he might surprise us. He's only a couple of years old and he's got a strong heart. The next twenty-four hours will be critical. If he survives until tomorrow night, then he should do okay. But he's going to need a lot of attention and love afterward."

"Carrie and I will make sure he gets it. Can we come see him?" She paused. "Do veterinary hospitals have visiting hours?"

"You can come anytime you like." He sighed and rubbed his hand along the back of his neck. He was tired and hungry.

"You were wonderful...." She seemed to sense his worry and exhaustion.

"Let's decide that in the morning."

"If Higgins lives, we'll owe everything to you."

"Higgins?"

"I thought it was a good name. Do you like it?"

He shrugged. He was too tired and too hungry to have much of an opinion on anything at the moment.

"You haven't had dinner, have you?" she surprised him by asking.

"No. How'd you know that?"

"You look hungry."

"That's because I am. You want to grab something?" he asked as if it were the most natural thing in the world.

She smiled. "Only this time I'll treat."

"Charlotte…"

"I insist. Please don't argue."

He didn't have the energy to protest, so he simply agreed. Since she was buying, he let her choose the restaurant. She decided on a nearby sandwich shop. He breathed in the scent of freshly baked bread as soon as he walked in the door.

It was the type of place where customers seated themselves and the silverware was wrapped in a red checkered napkin. The waitress, who looked all of sixteen, took their order, and promptly brought coffee. She came back a few minutes later with six-inch-high sandwiches, layered with sliced turkey, ham, roast beef, lettuce, tomato slices and onion.

"How have you been?" he asked casually after wolfing down the first half of his sandwich.

"Until the accident tonight I was just fine,"

Charlotte told him, her eyes flitting away
from his. "I don't know what came over me.
I'm usually not so emotional, but seeing that
poor little dog on the road bleeding and hurt
like that really got to me."

"It gets to me, too." The sight of an innocent animal suffering never failed to dis-
turb Jason, although he saw it time and time
again. The helplessness of the situation, the
complete disregard for life that a hit-and-run
accident revealed, angered him.

"I'm so glad you were home," Charlotte
said, keeping her gaze lowered. "I don't know
what I would have done otherwise."

"I'm glad I was there, too." He reached
across the table, taking her hand, linking their
fingers. Her skin was smooth and soft, just
the way he remembered.

His eyes sought hers. He smiled and she
smiled back. Jason felt ridiculously, unreasonably pleased that they were together. For
days he'd been fighting it, and now that they
were together, he felt foolish for having put
up such a struggle. He should quit worrying
about the future, he told himself. Live for the
moment. Wasn't that what all the self-help
books said? One day at a time. One kiss at
a time.

After what seemed like an eternity, Charlotte dragged her eyes from his.

"How about dessert?" he asked.

Charlotte picked up the menu and read over the limited selection.

"I was thinking more along the lines of homemade chocolate chip cookies," Jason said.

"They don't seem to have... Oh, you mean *mine?*" She raised eyes as blue as a summer sky.

He nodded enthusiastically. "I've reconsidered. It's true." His voice sounded slightly hoarse and, if he didn't know better, seductive.

"What is?"

"The way to my heart takes a direct route through my stomach."

"Oh." She blinked as if he'd caught her off guard. She was beautiful, he realized all over again. So gentle and caring. He'd missed her, yet he'd tried to convince himself otherwise, and had been doing a good job of it, too—too good, in fact.

The world seemed to stop. Jason knew his breathing did. He felt as if he were drowning in her eyes. He would've liked to blame it on how tired he was, but he'd only be lying to himself.

"You like softball?" he found himself asking next.

She nodded, obviously trying to keep her eyes averted from his. Apparently she was having a difficult time of it, because whenever their eyes met, it would be several moments before she looked away.

"I understand softball, more than basketball at any rate," she said, sounding slightly breathless.

"My brothers and I play on a team Saturday mornings. Do you and Carrie want to come and watch this weekend?"

Charlotte nodded.

"Good."

They were both silent on the way home. Jason knew he was going to kiss her again. He couldn't imagine *not* kissing her again.

Charlotte must have read his intentions, because her hand was on the car door the minute he shut off the engine. She reminded him of a trapped bird, eager to escape, and yet she didn't move.

His hand on her shoulder turned her toward him. His heart tripped wildly as she leaned toward him. He felt sure her heart was pounding as furiously as his.

Slowly, so slowly he wondered if he was dreaming it, Charlotte swayed closer. He lowered his mouth to hers. Jason wanted this kiss, wanted it more than he could remember wanting anything. It'd been over a week since he'd seen her and it felt like a lifetime. A thousand lifetimes.

Charlotte's hands were braced against his chest as he kissed her again, deeper, more fully. Again he kissed her, and again. Finally she broke away.

"Stop," she pleaded. The words were breathless and he could feel her shudder.

Reluctantly, Jason pulled back. Their eyes met again, and for the second time that night, Jason had the feeling she was frightened, although he didn't understand why. Wanting to comfort her, he traced a knuckle down the curve of her cheek.

"Carrie will be worried," she said.

He said nothing.

"I can't thank you enough. For saving Higgins. The dog."

Again Jason said nothing.

"Jason," she whispered. "Don't look at me like that."

"Like what?"

"Like you want to kiss me again."

"I do." He wasn't going to lie about it.

He saw that her hand was shaking as she opened the car door and climbed out. She seemed eager to make her escape now.

"Good night," she said with obvious false cheer.

"Little coward," Jason muttered under his breath, amused. "Saturday morning!" he shouted after her.

"What time?" She turned to face him again.

"Nine-thirty. Is that too early?"

"I'll be ready."

"I'll call you in the morning about Higgins."

"Please," she said, her eyes widening as though she'd momentarily forgotten the dog. "Oh, please do." She snapped open her purse and withdrew a business card, walking toward him now. "This is my number at the office. I'll be there after nine."

"Then I'll phone at nine."

"'Night."

"'Night," he echoed, returning to his apartment.

He wasn't there more than five minutes

when his doorbell chimed. He certainly wasn't in the mood for company, but as the building owner and manager, he couldn't very well ignore a visitor.

He opened his door to discover Carrie standing on the other side, a covered plastic bowl in her hand. "These are for you."

He accepted the container with a puzzled frown.

"Mom asked me to bring you some chocolate chip cookies," she said, grinning broadly.

Five

"Mom, you look fine."

"I don't look fine...I look wretched," Charlotte insisted, viewing her backside in the hallway mirror. She must've been mad to let Carrie talk her into buying jeans. Fashionably faded jeans, no less. Not only had she plunked down ninety bucks for the pair, they looked as if they'd spent the past ten years in someone's attic.

"You're acting like a little kid," Carrie said, slapping her hands against her sides in disgust. "We're going to a softball game, not the senior prom."

"Why didn't you tell me my thighs are so...round?" Charlotte cried in despair. "No woman wants to be seen in pants that make her legs look like hot dogs. I'm not going anywhere."

Carrie just rolled her eyes.

"Call Jason," Charlotte told her daughter. "Tell him…anything. Make up some excuse."

"You can't be serious."

"Please do as I say."

"Mom?"

"We're meeting his *family*," Charlotte cried. "I can't meet his brothers and sisters-in-law looking like this."

"Change clothes, then, if you're so self-conscious."

As though she had anything to change into. Charlotte's wardrobe was limited to business suits and sweatpants. There was no in-between. She couldn't afford to clothe both of them in expensive jeans. But after Jason had invited her out for today, she'd allowed Carrie to talk her into a shopping spree. Thank heaven for Visa. And thank heaven for Jason's generosity; he'd refused to accept any payment for the dog's care.

"I'm not calling Jason!" Carrie crossed her arms righteously. The girl had a streak of stubbornness a mile wide, and Charlotte had collided with it more than once.

Defeated, Charlotte muttered under her breath and fled to her room, sitting on the end of her bed. Before the shopping trip, she'd managed to put today's plans out of her mind and focus her attention on Higgins. Then the softball game had turned into the better part of a day, including a picnic, involving most of his family.

"Mom," Carrie said, approaching her carefully. "What's wrong?"

Charlotte shrugged, not sure how to explain her nervousness. "I wish I'd never agreed to this."

"But why?" Carrie wanted to know. "I've been looking forward to it all week. Just think of all the babysitting prospects. Jason's family is a potential gold mine for me." Carrie sat on the bed beside Charlotte. "We're going, aren't we?"

Charlotte nodded. She was overreacting, and she knew it. After shelling out ninety bucks she was wearing those jeans, no matter how they made her look.

"Good," Carrie said, leaping excitedly to her feet. "I've got the picnic basket packed. Honestly, Mom, we're bringing so much food, we could open a concession stand."

"I didn't want to run short." Charlotte didn't bother denying that she'd packed enough to feed Jason's entire family. A fruit-and-cheese plate, sandwiches, potato salad, a batch of chocolate chip cookies and a variety of other goodies she'd thrown in at the last minute.

Jason had casually mentioned the picnic the day before, when she'd gone to the hospital to visit Higgins. The dog was just beginning to respond to them. He was recovering slowly, but according to Jason, they'd be able to bring him home within a week. Charlotte soon discovered that visiting her new dog was a dual-edged sword. Every time she was at the veterinary hospital, she ran into Jason. Usually they had a cup of coffee together and talked; once he'd suggested dinner and Charlotte hadn't been able to dredge up a single excuse not to join him. He'd even taken her and Carrie to a movie. Now she was meeting his family, and it terrified her.

Ten minutes later, as Charlotte was rearranging their picnic basket to find room for a tablecloth and paper napkins, Jason arrived.

Carrie answered the door and directed him to the kitchen.

"Jason's here," she said unnecessarily.

"Hi." Charlotte greeted him nervously, turning around, a tense smile on her face. She was watching him carefully, wanting to read his expression when he saw her in the tight jeans.

"Hi, I was just—" He stopped abruptly, letting whatever he meant to say fade into nothingness. He stood before her, his mouth dangling open. Slowly his eyes widened.

With appreciation.

At least she thought it was appreciation. She prayed that was what it was, and not disgust or shock or any of the emotions she'd endured that morning.

"I...I've got everything ready." She rubbed her suddenly damp hands down her thighs. "Carrie says I've packed too much food, but I don't think so. I hope you like cantaloupe, because I just added one." She knew she was chattering aimlessly, but couldn't seem to stop.

"You look...fabulous."

"I do?" Charlotte hated how uncertain she sounded.

Jason nodded as though he wouldn't be able to take his eyes off her long enough to play ball, which had to be the nicest compliment he'd ever paid her.

"Carrie talked me into buying the jeans," she mumbled, tossing the napkins on top of the heap and closing the lid as far as it would go.

"Remind me to thank her."

He didn't say any more, just reached for the basket and brought it out to the car. Charlotte was so relieved, she wanted to weep with gratitude. Her spirits lifted—more than lifted—they soared as she and Carrie followed him. Carrie climbed in the backseat as Charlotte got in the front, hoping her jeans wouldn't split

The ball field was several miles away, near the Southcenter shopping mall. Charlotte was grateful to Carrie for carrying the conversation. Thrilled with the outing, the girl had plenty to say.

Charlotte had never been to this park before, and when she saw it she was astonished she hadn't heard of it. It had several baseball diamonds, and an equal number of soccer fields. The Green River intersected the park, with several footbridges spanning its banks.

"I didn't mention I was bringing anyone," Jason told her after he'd parked the car. "Everyone's going to ask you a bunch of embarrassing questions. Do you mind?"

"No," she answered, having trouble meeting his eyes. "Don't worry about it." She was a big girl—she could deal with a bit of curiosity.

"I don't usually bring someone."

Charlotte stiffened, not because she was timid or dreaded the questions, but because it confirmed something she'd rather not deal with right then. Jason was attracted to her. As attracted as she was to him.

What did bring fear to her heart was that he might be taking their time together seriously—that he might really start to care for her. That would be disastrous. *You care for him,* her heart reminded her. Yes, but that was different.

Kissing was all they'd done; it was all Charlotte had allowed. A few innocent kisses didn't amount to much. Or did they?

"Uncle Jase!" Two boys—Charlotte guessed they were seven or eight—raced across the green lawn toward Jason. One glance told her the pair were identical twins.

"Hello, boys," Jason said with a wide smile.

They stopped abruptly when they noticed Charlotte and Carrie, their eyes huge and questioning. Suspicious.

"These are my friends, Charlotte and Carrie," Jason said, motioning toward them.

"They're *girls,*" one of the pair muttered.

"I noticed that myself," a tall, athletic man said as he strode toward them. He was wearing the same uniform as Jason. Charlotte didn't need an introduction to know this was his brother.

"This is Paul, my oldest brother," Jason said, tucking a couple of baseball bats under his arm, along with his mitt. The task appeared to demand a great deal of attention.

In the next five minutes, Charlotte was introduced to Leah, Paul's wife, who was five months pregnant and chasing after a toddler named Kelsey. Jason's younger brother, Rich, his wife, Jamie, and their two children, Bethany and Jeremy, arrived shortly afterward, and there was another series of introductions.

Charlotte's head was spinning with all the names and faces. Everyone was friendly and helpful. Openly curious, too. Carrie, who loved children, was delighted when Rich's daughter wanted to sit in the bleachers with her.

The men were on the diamond warming up when Jamie sat next to Charlotte. Leah joined them, sitting on her other side. Charlotte smiled from one to the other. Their curiosity was almost visible. As the silence lengthened Charlotte frantically sorted through a number of possible topics, but try as she might, the most inventive thing she could think of was the weather.

Oh, what the heck, she decided. "I imagine you're curious about me," she said. After the morning she'd had, she wasn't up to a game of Twenty Questions.

"We didn't mean to be so blatant about it," Leah, the shorter of the two, murmured. She had one of the nicest smiles Charlotte had ever seen.

"You weren't," Charlotte lied.

"Yes, we were," Jamie said with a laugh. "We can't help it."

"Ask away," Charlotte invited.

"How long have you known Jason?" Rich's wife asked without hesitation.

Charlotte found Jamie Manning to be a study in contrasts. Rich, Jamie's husband, was probably one of the best-looking men she'd ever seen. Definitely *GQ* material. Yet, at first glance, his wife seemed rather plain. Charlotte soon learned how misleading first impressions could be. Five minutes with Jamie, and Charlotte was awed by her radiance. She had an inner glow that touched those around her.

"I met Jason about a year ago," Charlotte answered, when she realized both women were staring at her, waiting for her response.

"My daughter and I live in one of his apartments."

"A year," Jamie repeated, leaning forward so she could exchange a wide-eyed look with Leah. "Did you hear that? He's known her a whole year."

Charlotte felt she should explain further. "Actually, I met him a year ago, but we've only recently started to, uh, know each other."

"I see." Once again it was Leah who spoke, wearing a subtle smile as though she was amused and trying to disguise it.

"You'll have to forgive us for acting so surprised, but Jason doesn't usually bring anyone with him on Saturdays," Leah elaborated.

"Or any other day for that matter," Jamie added.

"So I understand. I…I take it he doesn't date often?" Charlotte asked. In some ways she was hoping they'd tell her he went through women like water. But in her heart she knew it wasn't true. If anything, it was just the opposite. Charlotte didn't want to hear that, either, didn't want to know she was special, because it made everything so much more difficult.

"Let's put it this way," Jamie answered, crossing her legs and resting her elbows on her knees. "We've been coming out here for what, two, three summers now, and this is the first time Jason's ever brought a woman."

Charlotte drew in a slow, deep breath.

"I don't remember Jason bringing a woman to any family function, ever," Leah said, looking positively delighted. Her eyes sparkled. "I'd say it was about time, wouldn't you, Jamie?"

"About time, indeed," Leah's sister-in-law said with a grin.

From his position on the diamond, Jason could see his two sisters-in-law on either side of Charlotte. No doubt they were pumping her for information, wanting to know every minute detail of their relationship. The distance was too great for him to be able to read Charlotte's expression.

If he had half a brain, he would've realized what he was doing before he invited her to join him. Why had he asked Charlotte to this game? Clearly he needed his head examined. Only an idiot would thrust a lamb like Charlotte into a pack of hounds without warning.

He'd told her his family would probably be curious about her, but he'd said it casually in the parking lot after they'd arrived. It wasn't like he'd given her much advance warning.

His family was far too nosy. By the end of the afternoon, Charlotte would be so sick of answering questions, she'd never want to go out with him again.

He pitched the ball to Paul with enough force to make his oldest brother remove his mitt, shake his hand and cast Jason an odd look.

Jason was angry. But it wasn't the way Leah and Jamie had surrounded Charlotte that had set him off. He'd had no business inviting Charlotte and Carrie to this game. For one thing, they were playing the league leaders and likely to be soundly defeated. If he was going to ask someone to come and watch them play ball, it should be against a team that'd make him look good, not like a bunch of fools. The outcome could prove to be downright embarrassing.

Not only were they likely to get their butts kicked, but Charlotte was going to spend the entire time being interrogated. First by Jamie and Leah, and then, when the game was over, by his brothers. They wouldn't be subtle about it, either. The first woman he'd cared about in years was going to come away thinking his family had been trained by the CIA.

Even now, Jason wasn't sure what had prompted him to ask Charlotte to come. But he certainly remembered the night he'd done it....

They'd been sitting in the car outside the apartment the night of Higgins's surgery. She'd been shaken by the accident, struggling to hide how much. He had known when he dropped her off that he was going to kiss her again. She'd known it, too. His lips had brushed hers. Lightly. Briefly. He had sensed she was still frightened—of him? Of their mutual passion? Of her own desires? Until she was at ease with him, he was content to proceed slowly. He'd never indulged in any kisses more sensual or seductive than those he'd shared with Charlotte.

He could tell she was a novice when it came to lovemaking. That surprised him because she'd been married. He'd never asked about her ex-husband, preferring to wait until she was comfortable enough to talk about it on her own. But from what Carrie had told him the day she'd come to his office, the marriage had been short and disastrous.

Jason was convinced Charlotte hadn't realized how much he enjoyed their kissing sessions. How much holding her satisfied him. How she left him feeling dizzy with need.

The same magic that had made him kiss her that night had encouraged him to risk inviting her to the ball game. Only now did he understand what he'd done. He'd dragged Charlotte into an impossible situation. Carrie, too. He was glad they were with him, but he wished he'd thought of some other way of introducing Charlotte and her daughter to his family. Some other time, when he'd be at her side to ward off their curiosity.

"Jase!" Rich's voice shot past his ear two seconds after a ball nearly creamed the side of his head.

Stunned, Jason took two steps backward.

"What's wrong with you?" Rich demanded furiously.

"You mean you don't know?" Paul shouted from the shortstop position. He looked pointedly toward the stands. "It seems to me that he's met his Waterloo."

After nearly getting his head knocked off by a fly ball, Jason focused his concentration on the game, which to his surprise wasn't going badly. Every now and then he could hear a high-pitched shout, which he'd like to think came from Charlotte. By the end of the seventh inning the score was tied.

Jason came to bat at the bottom of the ninth. The all-important ninth inning. The score remained tied and there were already two outs. Either he pulled off a hit or they were going into extra innings.

Charlotte was sitting in the stands almost directly behind him. He set the bat over his shoulder and eyed the pitcher. The first pitch was a fast ball and Jason swung, determined to hit it out of the field. More to the point, he was hoping not to be embarrassed in front of Charlotte.

He heard the cracking of the wood against the ball and he dropped the bat, then started running as though his life depended on making it to first base. It wasn't until he got there that he realized he'd hit a home run. He felt jubilant as he rounded the bases.

He cast his eyes toward the bleachers to find Charlotte on her feet, cheering and clapping. Her face was bright with excitement. In all his life, Jason had never felt such elation.

He crossed home plate and didn't stop. His brothers, his whole team, stared at him as he trotted behind the protective barrier between home plate and the viewing stands and headed straight for Charlotte. Excitedly, she launched herself into his arms.

Jason grabbed her around her waist, lifted her from the bleachers and swung her down. Her eyes shone with happiness and Jason thought he'd never seen a more beautiful woman.

Charlotte threw back her head and laughed. It wasn't for several minutes that Jason was even aware of the crowd that had gathered around them.

A bit self-conscious now, he lowered Charlotte to the ground, but kept his arm around her. Paul and Rich were the first to congratulate him, followed by several other teammates, who slapped him heartily on the back. One suggested Jason bring Charlotte again, since she was definitely his good-luck charm.

"You were wonderful," Charlotte said, smiling at him proudly. Jason found it difficult to pull his gaze away. The urge to kiss her was so strong, he had to fight to restrain himself. He would've done it, too, would've kissed her in front of everyone and ignored the consequences, if only his brothers hadn't been present. He held back more to protect Charlotte from embarrassment than to ward off any razzing he'd get from his family.

"I'm hungry," Ryan, one of the twins, announced once the excitement had died down. "When are we gonna eat?"

"Soon," Leah promised. Paul headed toward the parking lot.

"I'll be right back," Jason said and, without thinking, did the very thing he'd decided against. He kissed Charlotte briefly, before trailing after his brother to get the picnic basket in the trunk of his car.

Jason couldn't believe he'd done that. Neither could Charlotte, judging by the look of surprise that flashed in her blue eyes.

"Are you going to fess up?" Paul asked, holding a heavy cooler with both hands, studying Jason.

"To what?" he demanded, narrowing his eyes, hoping his brother would take the hint.

"Charlotte."

"What about her?"

"Don't go all defensive on me. I was just wondering how you met."

Jason relaxed a little. He was being too touchy. "She lives in the complex." He didn't think it would sound good if he admitted Carrie had offered him money to take her mother out.

"She seems nice."

"She is. Lay off her, though, will you?"

Paul's eyes went solemn, as if he was offended by Jason's remark. Then he nodded. "Whatever you want."

Paul must've said something to Rich, too, because when they sat down to eat, after pushing three picnic tables together, no one gave Charlotte more than a glance. It was as though she'd been part of the family for years. Which was just the way Jason wanted everyone to treat her. Heaven forbid she figure out how special she was to him. He'd already made a big enough fool of himself, simply by inviting her and Carrie to this outing.

Charlotte's daughter had won a few hearts all on her own, Jason saw, secretly pleased. Ryan and Ronnie had clamored to sit next to her at lunch, beating out Bethany, who cried with disappointment until Carrie agreed to hold the little girl on her lap.

"I think Carrie's made a conquest," Jason said to Charlotte, munching on a chocolate chip cookie. His fourth, and he was ready for another.

"She loves children. She's the type of kid who'd prefer to be the oldest of ten."

Jason watched as a sadness, however brief, flashed in Charlotte's eyes. It told him she wasn't speaking only for Carrie, but herself, as well. She must've wanted so much more from her marriage than she'd gotten. He remembered something else then, something Carrie had told him about Charlotte wanting more children. At the time he'd decided to stay away. A woman with marriage and children on her mind was someone he planned to avoid. Strangely, the thought didn't terrify him nearly as much now.

Still, he had to admit that the fleeting look of pain got to him. He'd experienced the desire to protect her in the past, to guard her from hurt, but only when she was in his arms. Only when he feared *he* might hurt her. Now, the need to keep her safe burned in his chest. He wanted to block out anything that would cause her pain. Most of all, he wanted to meet the ex-husband who'd walked away from his family, and he'd prefer it be in a dark alley some night.

Although he didn't know any details of the divorce, Carrie had told him she never heard from her father. What kind of man would desert his family? What kind of man would turn a warm, vivacious woman like Charlotte into a near-recluse?

"I like your family," Charlotte said, smiling up at him, distracting him from his thoughts.

"Did Leah and Jamie bombard you with questions?"

"A few, but they're so nice, I didn't mind."

"What did you tell them?" Jason was eager to know, partially because it might clear up a few questions he had himself. Maybe Charlotte could put into perspective what he was feeling and was unable to define.

She laughed, causing the others to momentarily look their way. "Are you worried?"

"No." The question surprised him.

"For a moment there, you looked as if you were afraid I might've told them something you'd rather I didn't."

"You can tell them anything you want," he said decisively, meaning it. If she chose to imply that they were madly in love, then fine, he'd deal with it. On the other hand, if she'd chosen to let his family believe they'd only just met, which wasn't so far from the truth, then he'd live with that, too.

"I told them we're friends…special friends."

Jason approved. He couldn't have said it better.

"Uncle Jase," Ronnie shouted, clutching a Frisbee. "Are we ready to play?"

"Play?" Jason didn't need to be invited twice. His favorite part of these family get-togethers was the time after lunch that he spent with his nieces and nephews. Chasing after Ronnie and Ryan and a Frisbee kept him young at heart, he told himself. Though he didn't care to admit out loud just how much he liked running around with a pair of eight-year-olds. The boys enjoyed it, too, and before the afternoon was over Rich and Paul invariably joined in.

As they did now. The two brothers against Jason and a handful of youngsters in a game of Frisbee football. A few minutes into the competition, Jason dived to catch a wild throw, catapulting himself into the air and latching triumphantly on to the disk.

Ronnie and Ryan cheered, and Jason felt as pleased with his small feat as he'd been with the home run. After an hour, the two teams took a break. Breathless, he reached for a cold soda, pulled back the tab and guzzled it down.

He turned, looking for Charlotte. The last time he'd seen her she was with Leah and Jamie cleaning up the remains of their picnic. He saw her sitting on a blanket under a madrona tree, bouncing Jeremy on her knee. Bethany and Kelsey were sprawled out, napping, beside her. She was playing a game with the baby, nuzzling his neck and making cooing sounds. Her eyes radiated a happiness he'd never seen. A joy that transfixed him.

"Jason, are you in or out?"

Jason barely heard the words, his gaze on Charlotte.

"In," he decided, tossing the empty can in the garbage and heading back to the field. A couple of minutes later he was completely engrossed in the game. Carrie had sided with his brothers against him and was proving to be a worthy opponent. Ronnie caught the Frisbee and lobbed it to his twin. Jason glanced toward Charlotte again and saw her lift Jeremy above her head and laugh up at him.

Jason's heart constricted. Watching Charlotte with his brother's child did funny things to his chest. She was smiling, happy. A powerful emotion seized his heart in a way that was almost painful.

One pain was followed almost immediately by another as the Frisbee hit him hard. The wind momentarily knocked out of him, he doubled over.

"Uncle Jase!"

"Jason!"

Paul and Ronnie were the first to reach him.

"You all right?" Paul asked.

Jason's eyes moved toward Charlotte and he shook his head. "No," he muttered, "I don't think I am."

Six

So this was what it meant to be part of a family, Charlotte mused, as Jason drove her and Carrie home from the ball field. This profound sense of belonging, of acceptance. She'd never experienced anything like it before. It was as though Jason's family had known and loved her for years. As though they genuinely cared for her. Charlotte couldn't recall a time when she'd felt anything as uplifting as she had that afternoon.

After the game they'd gathered together for a picnic. Charlotte didn't think she'd ever laughed more. There'd been good-natured teasing, jokes, games. Even now, driving home, laughter echoed in her ears. The cousins were as close as brothers and sisters, the older ones watching out for the smaller children. They fought like brothers and sisters, too, mostly over Carrie, each wanting her attention.

Carrie had beamed, loving every minute of it.

After the initial round of questions, Leah and Jamie had treated Charlotte like...well, like family. The women were obviously good friends, yet included Charlotte in all their conversations. Jason's brothers, too, had tried to make her feel comfortable. Neither Paul nor Rich had asked a single question about her relationship with Jason, probably content to have their wives fill in the gaps later.

"You're very quiet," Jason said, taking his eyes off the road for a second. "Anything wrong? My brothers didn't—"

"No," she assured him with a smile.

The only sound was the hum of the road. Carrie, usually filled with boundless energy, was exhausted after chasing the children around for most of the afternoon. She'd enjoyed herself as much as Charlotte had.

And perhaps her daughter was thinking the same thing Charlotte was—that she'd missed out on something important because they only had each other.

Jason parked the car, then carried the near-empty picnic basket into her kitchen. He hesitated after setting it on the counter. "You're *sure* nothing's wrong?"

Charlotte nodded. "Positive. I had a wonderful time. A fabulous time. Thank you for asking Carrie and me."

He didn't seem to believe her. "Did Leah and Jamie hound you with questions?" he asked for the second time that day, a pensive frown on his face.

"Jason," she murmured, resting her hands on his forearms and gazing up at him. "I meant it. Every word. This day with you and your brothers and their families was one of the happiest of my life. If I'm being introspective it's because...well, because I've never realized until now how much I've missed in life." Jason's questioning eyes sought hers, as if he wasn't sure he understood.

She managed to meet his eyes. She felt close to Jason just then, closer than she had to anyone, and that confused her. She was falling in love with this man and that was something she couldn't allow. Was it Jason she loved, or his family?

"Charlotte, look at me."

She ignored the request. "I was an only child, too," she told him, "like Carrie." She wanted to explain. "There were never outings that included aunts and uncles or cousins. This is a new experience for Carrie *and* me."

"Look at me," he said again, his voice low and commanding.

Slowly her gaze traveled the length of him, up his chest, over the width of his shoulders, to his eyes. She stared into them and felt a sudden sense of connection. It was a powerful sensation, powerful and exciting.

"Where's Carrie?" Jason asked, glancing over his shoulder.

"She's on the phone in her room. Why?"

"Because I'm going to kiss you."

Charlotte's heart tripped into double time. She was tempted to make some excuse, anything that would put an end to the craziness that overcame her with Jason, but she didn't trust her voice, let alone her heart.

Whatever she might've said was never meant to be. Jason's kiss saw to that. He gathered her in his arms, and lowered his mouth to hers. His lips were there, warm and moist, reminding her of sunshine. The kiss was chaste, yet curiously sensual.

Of her own accord she deepened their kiss. Jason responded quickly.

He moaned, or perhaps it was her own

voice making those soft sounds. She melted into him, her body responding instinctively, naturally, to his.

"Charlotte." He brought her even closer, and their kiss went on and on. She grew hot, and hotter, then hotter still…until…

"No more…" she cried, breaking away, panting. "Please…no more."

Jason trembled with restraint, closing his eyes. "You're right," he murmured. "Carrie's in the other room."

"Carrie," Charlotte repeated, grateful for the excuse.

Jason drew in several deep breaths, then said, "I should be leaving."

Charlotte nodded, but she didn't want him to go. Her body was on fire. She wondered if he was experiencing the same kind of torment himself—and if he was angry with her for sending him away.

"Would you like to come with me again next Saturday?" The question was offhanded, as though he'd just thought of it.

Charlotte's heart soared at the prospect. "If you're sure you want me."

Laughter leapt into his eyes, melding with the fire that was already there. "Trust me, Charlotte, I want you."

With that, he was out the door.

No sooner had Jason left than Carrie appeared in the kitchen. "Did Jason leave?"

Charlotte nodded, too preoccupied to answer outright. She was trembling, and all because of a few words. *He wanted her.* He'd been honest and forthright as she'd come to expect.

"Mom, we need to talk."

"Go ahead," Charlotte said, as she unloaded the picnic basket. There was surprisingly little food left over. Ryan and Ronnie had discovered her chocolate chip cookies, thanks to Jason, and the three dozen she'd brought had disappeared in no time. She'd set out the fresh fruit-and-cheese platter and that had disappeared, too. There were a couple of sandwiches still wrapped, but they'd keep for her and Carrie to eat the following day.

"It's about the ninth-grade dance," Carrie said stiffly from behind her.

Charlotte froze. This wasn't a subject she wanted to discuss, not again. "I've said everything I'm going to say about it, Carrie. The subject is closed."

"I hope you realize you're ruining my entire life," Carrie announced theatrically.

"Dropping you off at the dance and picking you up myself is a reasonable compromise, I think."

"Then you think wrong. I'd...rather walk to school naked than have you drive me to the dance as if...as if there wasn't a single boy in the entire class who wanted to be seen with me."

She sighed. "I'll be happy to pick up Brad, too, if that'll help." That was more than she was really in favor of, but she supposed she could live with it.

"Then everyone will think I asked Brad to the dance. I mean, I know girls do that, but it's important to me that a certain girl find out that Brad asked *me*. How can you do this, Mom? Can't you see how important this is?" Her eyes were imploring, a look designed to melt any mother's heart.

Charlotte steeled herself. "You're too young, Carrie, and that's the end of it."

"You don't understand what you're doing to me!" Carried wailed.

"The subject is closed."

"Fine, ruin my life. See if I care." She stalked out of the kitchen, arms swinging.

With a heavy sigh, Charlotte watched her go. This argument was getting old. She'd been under the impression that her daughter had accepted her decision. But now it was apparent Carrie had only been regrouping, altering her tactics. Cool reason had evolved into implied guilt. Her fifteen-year-old made it sound as though Charlotte had done untold psychological damage by not letting her go on an actual date. Well, so be it, Charlotte decided. This issue was one she didn't intend to back down on any more than she already had.

Pulling out a kitchen chair, Charlotte sank tiredly into it, resting her face in her hands. She sighed again. She had trouble enough raising one child; she was insane to even contemplate having another.

A baby.

But she *did* want another child, so badly she ached with it. Holding Jeremy, Jamie and Rich's little boy, had stirred to life a craving buried deep within her heart. She attempted to push the desire away, rebury it, anything but acknowledge it. She'd had to repress this desire several times over the years.

A baby now was out of the question, she stubbornly reminded herself. She was too old; there were dangers for a woman on the other side of thirty-five. But age was the least of her concerns.

Getting pregnant required a man. Even more problematic, it required making love.

The sadness that weighed down Charlotte's heart felt impossible to carry alone. Tears blurred her eyes. If ever there was a man she could love, it was Jason Manning. But the thought of falling in love again terrified her. Charlotte was afraid of love. Afraid of all the feelings and desires Jason had stirred to life. He was wonderful. His family was wonderful. But it was a painful kind of wonderful, taunting her with all that was never meant to be in her life.

Charlotte had dealt with her share of problems. Finances. Isolation. Low self-esteem. Everything had been a struggle for her. She didn't know how to react to *wonderful*.

For the first time since her divorce, Charlotte felt the protective walls she'd erected around her heart being threatened. Those barriers were fortified by years of disappointment, years of resentment and pain. Now they seemed to be crumbling and all because of a man she'd never even seen without a baseball cap.

For now, Jason was attracted to her, but in her heart she believed his interest in her wouldn't last. It couldn't. The time was fast approaching when she wouldn't be able to put him off, and he'd know. That very afternoon, she'd seen the way he'd trembled in an effort to restrain himself. She'd watched as he'd closed his eyes and drawn in several deep breaths.

Soon kissing wouldn't be enough for him. Soon he'd discover how inadequate she was when it came to making love. She had never satisfied Tom, no matter how hard she'd tried. In the end he'd taunted her, claiming the day would come when she'd realize all the ugly things he'd said about her were true. She didn't have what it took to satisfy a man.

When Jason learned that, he'd start to make excuses not to see her again. He'd regret ever having met her, and worse, he'd regret having introduced her to his family.

She never should've accepted his invitation. It would make everything so much more awkward later....

The tears slipped from her eyes before she was aware she was crying. The soul-deep insecurity, awakened by the memories of her marriage, returned to haunt her. The doubts, the fear and dread, were back, taking up residence in her mind.

Covering her face with her hands, Charlotte swallowed the sobs beginning to spill out in huge swells of emotion. In an effort to gain control, she held her breath so long her lungs ached.

She heard her ex-husband's words—*you aren't woman enough*—inflicting injury all over again until she covered her ears and closed her eyes, wanting to blot them out forever.

Why should Jason fall in love with her when the world was full of whole, sexual women who'd gladly satisfy his needs? Passionate women who'd blossom in his arms and sigh with pleasure and fulfillment. She was incapable of giving a man what he needed. Tom had repeatedly told her so. She was inept as a woman, inept at lovemaking.

"Mom," Carrie said coolly from behind her. "I'm going to Amanda's house." She waited as though she expected Charlotte to object.

Charlotte nodded, then stood and resumed unpacking the picnic basket, not wanting Carrie to see her tears. "Okay, honey. Just don't be late."

"I may never come home again," Carrie said dramatically.

"Dinner's at six."

"All right," Carrie muttered and walked out the door.

It wasn't until later, much later, while she was in bed finding it impossible to sleep, that Charlotte's thoughts returned to Jason. She'd allowed things to go further than she should have. It was a mistake. One she had to correct at the earliest possible moment. She must've been crazy to let their relationship reach this point.

Crazy or desperate? Charlotte didn't know which. It had all started weeks earlier when she'd held a friend's baby. Funny how she could remember the precise moment with such accuracy. The longing for a child had escalated within her, gaining momentum, refusing to be ignored. She'd gone home and wept and although the tears had finally dried, inside she hadn't stopped weeping.

Shortly after the incident with Kathy Crenshaw and her baby, Charlotte had met Jason. He'd kissed her that first night and it had been… She hadn't tensed or frozen up and that had given her hope. Her confidence continued to grow when he kissed her again and again; he'd always been gentle and undemanding. He was special that way, and she'd be forever grateful for the uncanny gift he had of understanding her needs.

But Jason was a man of raw sensuality. He wouldn't be satisfied with a few chaste kisses for much longer. He had no idea how terrified she was of him, of any man.

No, it was only a matter of time before the best thing that had happened to her in years came abruptly to an end.

On Sunday, Jason wasn't in the mood to cook. Microwave popcorn for dinner suited him better than a frozen entrée. He popped a batch and sat down in front of the television to watch a bowling tournament. Not his favorite sport, but there wasn't much to choose from.

When his phone rang, he stood on the sofa and reached across to grab it from the kitchen counter. He was half hoping it was Charlotte.

It wasn't.

"Jase, I don't suppose you've got Charlotte's phone number, do you?" Paul asked cordially enough, only Jason wasn't fooled. As the oldest, his brother sometimes got the notion that he needed to oversee family matters. That didn't include Charlotte, and Jason intended to make sure Paul understood that.

"Jase?"

Of course he had Charlotte's number. "Yeah. What do you want it for?" Suspicions multiplied in his brain. Being a newspaper reporter, Paul was used to getting information out of people.

"Don't get all bent out of shape, little brother. Leah and I want to go to a movie."

"So?"

"So, we'd like Carrie to babysit. She was a real hit with the boys yesterday. You don't mind, do you? The girl's a natural with kids."

"Of course I don't mind." The fact was, Jason felt downright pleased. If Paul and Leah wanted Carrie to babysit, then Charlotte would be at home alone. He could come up with an excuse—Higgins would do—and casually drop in on her.

They needed to talk, and the sooner the better, although it wasn't talking that interested him.

He tossed what remained of his popcorn in the garbage, brushed his teeth and shaved. He even slapped on some cologne. He wasn't accustomed to using anything more than aftershave, but this evening was an exception.

He was whistling when he'd finished, his spirits high.

On the pretense of asking about next Saturday's ball game, he phoned his brother to be certain Paul had managed to get hold of Carrie. He had. In fact, he'd be picking her up in the next half hour. Allowing ten minutes for Paul to whisk Carrie out of the apartment, that left him with forty minutes to kill.

Forty minutes would go fast, Jason mused, as he sat back down and turned on the TV. But his mind wasn't on the bowling match. A far more intriguing match was playing in his mind. One between Charlotte and him.

Tonight was the night, he decided, determined to take Charlotte beyond the kissing stage. He didn't mean to be calculating and devious about it... Well, yes, he did, Jason thought with a grin.

He'd be gentle with her, he promised himself. Patient and reassuring. For years he'd been treating terrified animals. One stubborn woman shouldn't be any more difficult. He had no intention of pressuring her into anything. Nor would he coerce her if she was at all uncomfortable. He'd lead into lovemaking naturally, spontaneously.

He glanced at his watch, eager now, and was disappointed to see that only ten minutes had passed. Half an hour wasn't *really* very long, but it seemed to feel that way to Jason.

"I'm leaving now, Mom," Carrie called out.

Charlotte walked out of the kitchen, drying her hands on a terry-cloth towel. She smiled at Paul, then looked at her daughter. "Do you know what time you'll be home?"

"Before ten. Don't worry, I know it's a school night."

"I'll have her back closer to nine," Paul assured Charlotte.

"Okay." She nodded. "Have fun."

"I will," Carrie said as they left, offering her first smile of the day. Actually, Charlotte had been talking to Paul, but she let it pass. Carrie was still upset about the school dance and had been cool toward Charlotte all afternoon.

Charlotte had just settled down with a book when there was a knock at the door. *Please, God, don't let it be Jason,* she prayed, but apparently God was occupied elsewhere. Just as she'd feared, she opened the door and came face-to-face with Jason, boyishly handsome in his baseball cap.

"Hi," he said, charming her with his smile. It wasn't fair that a man should be able to wreak such havoc on a woman's heart with a mere movement of the lips.

"Hello." She'd been dreading this moment all day. "I was going to phone you later." A slight exaggeration; she'd been planning to delay calling for as long as possible.

"Oh?"

"Yes...I won't be able to go to the ball game with you next Saturday after all."

"Don't worry about it," he said, making himself comfortable on her sofa. He anchored his ankle on the opposite knee and grinned up at her. "There'll be plenty of other Saturdays. The summer is filled with Saturdays."

It was awkward for her to be standing, while he seemed completely at home. So Charlotte sat, too—as far away from him as she could while still being on the same sofa. She angled her legs sideways, her hands clasped. "I'm afraid I won't be able to make it any other Saturday, either."

A pause followed her announcement. "Why not?"

"I...I..." She couldn't look at him. "I don't

think it's a good idea for us to see each other anymore."

"Uh-huh." He didn't reveal his reactions one way or another.

Emotion seemed to thicken the air. He might not be *saying* anything, but he was feeling it. Charlotte was, too.

"Is it something I said?"

She lowered her eyes farther and shook her head.

"Something I did?"

"No... Oh, please, Jason, just accept this. Don't make it any more difficult than it already is." Her voice, which had remained steady until then, cracked.

"Charlotte," Jason said, moving next to her with startling agility. "For heaven's sake, what's wrong?"

She covered her mouth with one hand and closed her eyes.

"I'm not leaving until you tell me," he said.

"I can't."

"Why can't you?"

"Because!" she cried, leaping to her feet. "Everything would've been all right if you hadn't been so...so nice." She was angry now, unreasonably angry, and not quite sure why.

Jason stood, too, his gaze holding hers.

"I'm not sorry I kissed you. Nothing would make me regret that."

His words made it all so difficult. She wasn't sorry, either.

Her expression must have told him as much. He relaxed visibly and reached for her, gently holding her shoulders. Slowly, he drew her forward. Charlotte had no resistance left, and walked right into his embrace.

She sobbed once, then hid her face in his chest and wept openly.

Jason stroked her hair and whispered reassurances in her ear, as if she were a small child needing comforting. In some ways, she was exactly that.

After several minutes he lifted her face upward to meet his mouth. Over and over again he kissed her, lightly, softly, gently. Her breathing grew shallow.

"Jason…"

"Yes?" He raised his head, his eyes meeting hers.

"You're doing it again."

His mouth curved into a deliberate smile. "I know."

Her hands were against his chest when he sought her mouth again. He was still gentle, but the kisses changed in texture and intensity. Their lips were fused together, the heat between them burning so fierce, she thought it might scorch her. Charlotte found it difficult to breathe, but she didn't care. Breathing wasn't important. She held on, her hands clutching his upper arms.

Jason led her back to the sofa, and without protest, Charlotte followed. He sat down and brought her into his lap. He didn't give her the opportunity to protest before he directed her lips back to his. When her mouth opened in exultant welcome, he moaned. He kissed her again and again, until she was panting. Until her heart seemed to stop beating. Until there was nothing in her world but him.

His hands were opening the front of her blouse even before she realized his intent.

"Jason, no," she said in a panic. "Please, no."

"All right." Jason twisted around and turned off the light. The room dimmed and shadows danced across the walls. "Is this better?" he asked.

Charlotte clamped her eyes shut. "I…I'm not very good at this," she whispered, close to tears. "I'm not…sexy enough." The only thing that kept her from springing free of his hold was fear. It held her immobile.

"You're beautiful," he whispered. "Charlotte, do you hear me? You're perfect."

She buried her hands in his hair. His cap was gone, but she didn't remember when he'd removed it. Or if he had. She sighed.

He kissed her again, his mouth hard and hungry. Charlotte understood his hunger, but she wasn't capable of satisfying it. "No," she whispered when she could.

"No?" How disappointed he sounded.

"No," she said a second time.

"You're sure of that?" he asked, sounding regretful.

"Y-yes."

He nodded, kissed her once more, then inhaled sharply. "I just wanted to check."

Seven

"Who told you that you aren't sexy?" Jason asked, relaxing on her sofa.

Charlotte's hands stilled as she poured coffee into two mugs.

How do you expect a man to get excited when his wife's such a cold fish? No wonder you're a failure at lovemaking. Are you sure you're even a woman?

Charlotte's heart reeled as Tom's words returned to haunt her. She'd laid to rest as much of his vindictiveness as she could, bound her wounds and gone on with her life. Pulling away the bandage, examining the damage now, just seemed pointless.

"Charlotte?" he probed gently.

"My ex-husband," she muttered.

"He's wrong, you know."

She nodded, rather than argue with Jason.

For the moment he was infatuated with her, but his fascination wouldn't last, and eventually he'd feel the same way as Tom.

"You never mention your ex-husband."

"There's not much to say." She carried the two mugs into the living room. "Carrie was excited about babysitting Paul and Leah's children," she said, pointedly changing the subject.

Jason stood and took a cup from her hands, then sat next to her on the sofa, sliding his arm around her shoulders. His touch was warm against her chilled skin.

"You're perfect," he whispered and kissed her cheek. "You're lovely and sensuous and beautiful. Don't ever let anyone tell you differently. I'm not going to force you to discuss your marriage. Not now, but I want you to know I'll be ready to listen whenever you're ready to talk."

She smiled wanly, determined to steer the conversation away from the past.

Jason drank his coffee and left soon afterward, when it was apparent Charlotte wasn't in the mood to talk. She wasn't sure *what* her mood was, but she lacked the strength to analyze it.

Before leaving, Jason asked if she'd changed

her mind again about the ball game on Saturday, and after a short hesitation, she nodded. Yes, she'd go, she told him. Jason smiled, obviously pleased, and headed out the door.

Something was happening to her, Charlotte thought, trembling. And it was happening against her will.

She'd made the decision earlier—she wasn't going to see him again. After careful deliberation she'd decided it was best to end everything now before one or both of them ended up hurt. It was a simple, cut-and-dried conclusion.

Yet...yet when she'd tried to talk to him about it, regret and doubt had consumed her until she'd dissolved in tears and pain.

Heaven help her, she didn't want it to end! Jason must've sensed that because he hadn't appeared too concerned when she'd told him.

His confidence was well-founded. Within minutes, he'd broken through her resolve and was kissing her senseless. And Charlotte hadn't raised a single objection.

It was too late. Too late to walk away from him. Too late to go back to the way her life had been before Jason. She was trapped by her own weakness and would continue to be until Jason discovered the truth for himself.

Carrie arrived home soon afterward, full of tales about the twins and Kelsey. Seconds later, it seemed, she was in her room and on the phone. Her thoughts heavy, Charlotte appreciated the privacy.

It wasn't as though this was the first time Jason had kissed her. The impact he had on her senses wasn't startling or new. The man had the uncanny knack of stirring awake the part of her she'd thought had died the day Tom asked for a divorce.

She felt reborn, alive with hope. And yet she was more frightened than she'd ever been before. Everything was different with Jason. In his arms she experienced an excitement she'd never even known was possible. His tenderness, the loving gentle way in which he touched her, had given her cause to wonder, for the first time, if what Tom had said was true.

What if it wasn't? Could that be possible? With Jason she felt none of the dread she'd felt when Tom had kissed her. His lovemaking had always been so hurried, so raw, as if he were in a rush to complete the act so he could turn away from her. She couldn't imagine Jason being anything but compassionate and tender.

But what if all the things Tom had said *were* true? Her heart slowed with uneasiness. Jason Manning was an attractive, sensual man. A passionate man. And he'd expect— no, he'd need—a passionate woman.

Thinking of her years with Tom conjured up such ugly images in her mind. His taunts echoed like the constant sound of waves in a seashell, never stopping, never fading, always there to remind her of what a failure she was.

At ten, Charlotte turned out the lights, made sure Carrie was off the phone and went to bed. She should've guessed that sleep would escape her that night.

You're perfect, Jason had said.

Only she wasn't—Tom had made certain she knew as much. The need to weep welled up within her, tightening her throat.

She had loved Tom. She'd hated him.

He had stripped her of her pride when he left.

Her life had ended that day. Yet, in other ways, her life had begun.

She'd known for weeks, months, that Tom was involved with another woman, and she'd said nothing because she was afraid. Because she feared life alone. Because she was will- ing to do whatever she could to save her marriage, even if that meant denying the truth. So she'd chosen to believe his lies.

When he'd forced her to face reality, he'd come at her in anger and guilt...and hate. She hadn't cried. Not a single tear, not even when the divorce was decreed final. It wasn't until years later that she gave herself permission to grieve for the marriage, the fantasy she'd built in her mind of what might have been.

In the beginning she'd been too numb with shock, too dazed by that last horrible scene, to experience any emotion. Gradually, as time passed, Charlotte began to feel again, a little at a time. It was like an anesthetic wearing off. As the years went by, as the numbness faded, she had to deal with the pain. A throbbing, savage pain.

Her grief came in waves. Regret struck first, reminding her of all the might-have-beens; one fantasy led to another. By now they would've had more children, she'd told herself. Tom would be established in his career and she'd be living the life she'd been cheated of as a child.

Anger followed regret. How could she have given her heart to a man who'd ravaged her self-respect? How could she have loved him when he'd treated her so poorly? But love him she had, so much that she still ached at losing the life she'd dreamed they'd share.

But mostly, as the years went on, Charlotte felt an overwhelming sense of guilt. She knew it was unreasonable. After all, it was Tom who'd cheated on her, Tom who'd walked out on his family, abandoned his wife and child. It was Tom who'd forsaken their vows. Yet *she* was the one who accepted responsibility.

Sometimes the guilt was so overpowering, Charlotte found it intolerable. If she'd been a better wife, Tom wouldn't have sought another woman. He'd said so himself. If she'd been more enticing, more sexual, more attractive, more satisfying, he wouldn't have done it. She was too thin, too flat, too cold. The list was endless.

After years of telling herself that Tom had used her inadequacies as an excuse for adultery, years of struggling to repair her self-esteem, Charlotte gave up. Surrendered. She bought it all. The reassurances she tried to offer herself were empty. Null and void.

Everything Tom had said was true. She was a failure as a woman. A failure as a wife. No man would ever be satisfied with her. Not for long. Tom hadn't been and Jason wouldn't be, either. She might as well accept that now and stop fighting the inevitable.

The doorbell chimed just as Jason finished reading the latest issue of one of the veterinary periodicals he subscribed to.

"Yeah?" he said, opening the door, half expecting one of his tenants.

"Hi," Carrie said, striding purposefully into his apartment. "Have you got a minute to talk?"

"Sure." Jason led the way into the living room and sat down. Carrie started to pace in front of his television, hands behind her back. Walking in his apartment was dangerous with the week's worth of newspapers spread across the carpet.

"Is it Higgins?" he prompted, when she didn't speak right away.

She shook her head, eyes lighting up. "Higgins is doing great. He's eating and everything. I think he likes it with Mom and me."

"I'm sure he does." They'd lavished the dog with love and attention from the moment Jason had carried him into their apartment on Monday afternoon. One would've thought the mutt was some kind of hero. In a way he was, Jason decided. If it hadn't been for the dog,

Jason didn't know how long it would have taken him and Charlotte to connect.

"What can I do for you?"

"It's Mom," Carrie said.

"What about your mother?" He saw that tears had pooled in Carrie's eyes, and she wasn't trying to hide the fact. Like most men, Jason was uncomfortable when a woman started to cry. No matter what the cause, he felt personally responsible. And he felt an overpowering urge to do whatever he could to rectify the problem.

He certainly felt that way with Charlotte— even more so. She'd look at him with her beautiful blue eyes and the instant he saw the slightest hint of tears, he'd be putty in her hands. He was putty in her hands, anyway, tears or not, but that was because it was Charlotte.

"My mother's ruining my life," Carrie was saying.

Jason was no psychiatrist, but he wasn't completely obtuse. "Does this have something to do with that dance?"

Carrie nodded. "There's this boy…his name's Brad. He's the cutest boy in class and the star of the track team. Every girl in school's crazy about him and he asked *me*.

Me," she emphasized again, bringing her hand to her heart. "He asked me to the ninth-grade dance. When I talked to Mom, she said I could go, but when I said Brad's father was picking us up and…and driving us there, she went totally weird on me."

"I'm sure your mother has a good reason for feeling the way she does."

"She won't even talk about it."

"Carrie, listen. I'd like to help, but this is between you and your mother. I can't interfere with a parenting decision."

Carrie nodded, her throat working as she struggled not to cry. "I don't expect you to interfere… I was hoping that you'd help me—tell me what to say to make Mom understand how old-fashioned she's being. I haven't said anything to Brad about my mom not wanting me to be in the same car as him and his dad and…and the dance is next Friday night. There isn't much time left."

Jason rubbed the side of his face. "What's your mother's primary objection?"

"She thinks driving with him makes it a real date. And I'm not allowed to *date* until next year."

"I see. What if she drove you and Brad to the dance?"

"That won't work, either.... Everyone will think I asked him and...it might be silly, but I want Suzie Jennings to know otherwise." She wiped her eyes and took a moment to regain her composure.

"How about if Brad's dad drops you off and your mother picks the two of you up after the dance?"

Carrie dropped her hands to her side. "Picks us up?" she repeated thoughtfully.

"It wouldn't be considered a date then, would it? The two of you obviously need to be driven to and from the dance and this would simply be a means of transporting you."

"There's a party at Amanda Emerich's house right afterward, but it's directly across the street from the school and everyone's invited."

"I have an even better idea," Jason said enthusiastically. At Carrie's blank stare, he explained. "How about if your mother offered to chaperone the dance?"

Judging by the look Carrie gave him, she didn't share his enthusiasm. "That wouldn't work because she'd need a date. Chaperones at our school dances are always couples."

"I'll go with her," Jason said casually. As soon as he made the suggestion, he wanted to jerk it back. Him dancing? The last dance he'd attended had been his sister's engagement party. He'd rented a tuxedo and been miserable most of the night. Before then, his only other experience on the dance floor had been as a high-school junior. He didn't know how to dance then and he hadn't learned since.

"You'd do that?" Carrie asked, her voice rising. For the first time since she'd entered his home, her eyes sparkled with hope.

"Ah…" Oh, what the heck, he'd do it if it would help the kid. "Sure," he answered. "I'd volunteer to be a chaperone."

Carrie let out a cry of glee and raced across the room to throw her arms around his neck.

"Your mother might not be willing—"

"She will," Carrie said confidently. "Mom's crazy about you."

"Yes, but will she be crazy about the idea of Brad's dad driving you there and the two of us taking you home?"

Carrie mulled that over for a moment. "Of course she will," she said, revealing no doubt. "Why shouldn't she be? It's a wonderful compromise. We'll both be satisfied…. I mean, this plan isn't perfect—no one wants their mother chaperoning a school dance—but it'll work because Mom's going to agree when she knows you suggested it."

Jason was suffering from second thoughts when he rang Charlotte's doorbell an hour later. Carrie had devised a plan for approaching Charlotte with his idea. At the appropriate point, he was to suggest the two of them chaperone the dance and make it sound like a spur-of-the-moment idea.

He was rather proud of his compromise— not the part about chaperoning the dance, but the shared-driving idea. By the time Carrie had left his apartment, he felt like an expert. Raising children wasn't so difficult if you applied a bit of common sense.

Now, though, he wasn't entirely sure he should get involved. The dance was an issue between Charlotte and Carrie, and his instincts told him he was trespassing.

It would've been different if Charlotte had come to him for advice, but she hadn't and he doubted she would. There wasn't any reason for her to, at least not with regard to Carrie. Charlotte was the one with parenting experience, not him.

Despite his second thoughts over his role in this drama, he'd agreed to help Carrie—

even though his instincts now told him he was going to regret this.

Carrie answered the doorbell and smiled brightly when she saw him.

Charlotte looked pleased to see him, too, but she also looked like she'd rather not be. Jason was learning to read her quite well, and that skill was coming in handy.

"Hello, Jason," she said softly.

"Hi. I stopped by to see how Higgins is doing." A weak excuse, and one she was bound to see through in the next couple of minutes.

The black dog trotted toward him, his tail wagging slowly. Jason squatted beside him and affectionately rubbed his ears. "How do you like your new home, fellow?" he asked.

"Do you want a cup of coffee?" Carrie called out from the kitchen. Her voice was enthusiastic. The kid wasn't any better at disguising her emotions than her mother was.

"Please." Jason glanced up at Charlotte. He didn't know what was going on with her lately. She'd been avoiding him—that much he understood—but he was willing to give her the space she needed. For now. He was a patient man. She was attracted to him, fighting it as hard as she could, but her resistance wasn't strong enough to defeat him.

For the first time in his life, Jason had met a woman who needed him. Unfortunately she was too self-sufficient and proud to admit it. Charlotte Weston brought out all his protective urges. And his intuition told him he'd begun to bring out qualities in her—a sensual confidence and an ability to laugh, have fun—that she'd been repressing for years.

The woman was a puzzle, but slowly, surely, he was putting together the various pieces she revealed. Once he had the whole picture, he'd be able to scale those defensive walls of hers.

He strongly suspected Charlotte's problems revolved around her ex-husband and her marriage. She'd been badly hurt, and gaining her trust and her love would require time and patience. Where Charlotte was concerned, Jason had an abundant supply of both. Carrie brought him a cup of coffee, and Jason pulled out a kitchen chair, then nonchalantly sat down. Carrie did the same. Higgins ambled over and settled at his feet.

Charlotte glanced at the two of them and frowned. "Is something going on here that I should know about?"

The kid couldn't have been more obvious, Jason mused again. "Carrie came to me earlier this afternoon," he announced, deciding honesty was the best policy, after all. The way he figured, if they were forthright about *what* they'd discussed, then Charlotte might be willing to forgive them for discussing it behind her back.

"Jason," Carrie muttered a warning under her breath.

"Carrie came to you?" Charlotte demanded. "About what?"

"The dance," Carrie admitted sheepishly.

"You went to Jason about an issue that's strictly between you and me?"

"I needed to talk to someone," Carrie cried, pushing back the chair when she stood. She faced her mother, feet braced apart, hands on her hips. "You're being completely unreasonable and Jason agrees with me. He came up with—"

"Carrie." Jason could see he'd been wrong. In this case, honesty might not have been the best policy. "I didn't ever say I thought your mother was unreasonable."

His defense came too late. Charlotte whirled on him, her face red and growing redder. Her eyes, the eyes he'd always found so intriguing, were filled with disdain.

"Who gave you the right to intrude in my life?" she flared.

"Charlotte, it's not what you think." Jason could feel himself sinking waist-deep in the quicksand of regret.

"You're undermining my authority."

"Mom...please, hear me out."

"Charlotte, give me a chance to explain." Jason didn't have much of an argument; he should've listened to his instincts and stayed out of this.

"You may think because...because I've let you get close to Carrie and me that you have the right to express your opinion on how she should be raised, but you're wrong. What goes on between my daughter and me is none of your business. Do I make myself clear?"

Feeling all the more chagrined, Jason nodded. The best thing to do now was make a hasty retreat. "I can see I've—"

"Just go." Charlotte's voice trembled as she pointed to her door.

"Mom," Carrie shouted. "The least you can do is listen to him."

Charlotte ignored her daughter while Jason, calling himself every kind of fool, made his way out of the apartment. He paused long enough to cast an apologetic glance at Carrie, but he agreed with Charlotte. He'd butted in where he didn't belong.

After Jason's departure, Carrie went to her room, slamming her door with such force Higgins scrambled across the living room, frantically looking for a place to hide.

Charlotte was so angry, it was all she could do not to follow Jason and tell him she never wanted to see him again. She would have done it, too, if she didn't know she'd regret it later. And if she didn't need to coax Higgins out from behind the couch and comfort him.

The man had some nerve! If Carrie thought she was going to manipulate her into giving in by getting Jason to side with her, then her daughter was wrong.

"I hope you realize what you've just done!" Carrie shouted as she opened her door.

Still stroking Higgins, Charlotte ignored her.

"You've insulted Jason."

"He deserved it."

"Like hell."

"Watch your language, young lady."

* * *

Thirty silent minutes passed while Charlotte cooled her temper. Carrie was apparently doing the same thing. A short while later, her bedroom door opened again and she walked out. She was pale and her eyes showed evidence of crying, but she appeared to have composed herself.

The same didn't hold true for Charlotte. She was still furious. How dare Jason involve himself in her affairs!

"I've called Brad," Carrie announced, opening the refrigerator. She stared at the contents, took out a cold pop and pulled back the tab. After taking one long drink, she turned to face Charlotte. "Brad said he'd tell his dad you'd be driving us to and from the dance."

Of all the things Charlotte might have expected, this wasn't one. "Good," she said, feeling only a little better.

"I...was hoping you'd be willing to split the duties. Let Brad's father drive us there and you pick us up."

Charlotte mulled it over. That didn't sound so unreasonable. She'd have a chance to meet the boy's father when he came to get Carrie, and it wasn't as if the two kids would be alone in the car—or at the dance.

"I...I'd be willing to agree to that."

Charlotte thought Carrie would be grateful or relieved; instead she broke into giant hiccuping sobs. Her daughter slumped in a kitchen chair and buried her face in her arms and wept as if she'd lost her best friend.

"Carrie." Charlotte placed her hand on Carrie's shoulder. "What's wrong?"

She raised her head and brushed the tears from her face, her shoulders heaving with the effort to stop crying. "You should never have said those things to Jason."

"Carrie, he intruded in my affairs."

"But I was the one who asked him to talk to you. If you're going to be angry with anyone, it should be me, not him."

Charlotte realized Carrie didn't understand the nuances of a male-female relationship. Frankly, she wasn't that well acquainted with them herself. She'd admit that she'd reacted in anger, but it was justified. Jason had simply assumed too much.

"But Jason didn't want to interfere," Carrie sobbed. "It took me forever to get him to agree and...and he only did it because I was desperate."

"He overstepped the bounds." Charlotte tried to remain adamant.

"You made him leave without even bothering to listen."

Charlotte said nothing.

"I like Jason—and you do, too," Carrie added unnecessarily. "He's the best thing that's ever happened to us. Higgins is alive because of him and…and he took us to meet his family. Saturday was the most fun day I've ever had. It…it was like we belonged with Jason and his brothers."

Charlotte had felt the same way.

"Jason wasn't minding your business, Mom, at least not the way you think. He… he was helping a friend. Me. And you hated him for that."

"I don't hate Jason." Far from it. She was falling in love with him.

"He's the one who came up with the idea of Brad's father driving one way and you driving the other. He…he suggested you chaperone the dance just so you'd feel comfortable about everything." She drew in a shaky breath. "When I told him you'd need a date for the dance if you were going to be a chaperone, he said *he'd* take you. I mean, Jason isn't the kind of man who dances…but he'd be willing to do it, for me, because he's my friend. And for you, too, so you'd be comfortable at the dance. And what did he get for being so nice?"

"My anger," Charlotte whispered, feeling wretched.

"You kicked him out of the house, and I don't think he'll ever want to come back. I know I wouldn't."

Charlotte sat down next to her daughter, feeling strangely like weeping herself.

"I wanted to go to the dance with Brad more than anything," Carrie admitted, "but now I don't care if I do or not."

"Carrie, this isn't the end of the world."

"I *really* like Jason," she said emphatically. "When I asked him if he'd ask you out, I did it for selfish reasons, and I apologize for that... but I'm glad I did it. You're happier when you're with him, Mom. You don't think I notice, but I do. Jason makes you smile and laugh and forget how much you don't like your job."

Charlotte folded her arms around her middle. What Carrie said was true. It was as if her life had started all over again when Jason first kissed her.

"I don't care about the dance anymore,"

Carrie murmured. "But I care what happens with you and Jason. Go to him, Mom. Tell him you're sorry. Please."

Her daughter's entreaty affected Charlotte more than any regrets she might feel about what she'd said and done. For one thing, she hadn't realized how fond Carrie was of Jason.

"Will you do it, Mom?"

It didn't take Charlotte long to decide. "Yes," she said. She would apologize, for not giving him the benefit of the doubt, for not being willing to listen to him and Carrie, but mostly for the rude way in which she'd told him to leave her apartment.

It was the second time she'd had to apologize to this man.

"When?" Carrie asked.

"Soon," Charlotte promised.

The opportunity came the following morning. After walking Higgins, Charlotte was on her way to the office, crossing the parking lot. She'd spent a sleepless night composing what she intended to say to Jason. She'd wait until that evening, go to his apartment and say what needed to be said.

She was halfway to her car when she heard

her name. Her heart filled with dread when she saw Jason jogging toward her.

"Hello," she said, feeling wretched.

"I won't keep you." His eyes bored into hers. "I want you to know I'm sorry for what happened yesterday. I should never have gotten involved. This is between you and Carrie, and I was out of line."

"I should never have spoken to you the way I did."

"You were angry and you had every right to be."

"But you... Oh, Jason, I feel terrible."

He frowned. "Why should you?"

"Carrie told me how you were willing to help chaperone the dance and...and I didn't have the common decency to hear you out."

"It's probably for the best. I'm not much of a dancer."

Charlotte smiled up at him, knowing her heart shone in her eyes, and not caring. "Why don't you let me find that out for myself Friday night?"

Eight

"You need to borrow a suit?" Rich asked, looking smugly amused as he led Jason to the walk-in closet in the huge master bedroom. The home had been built several years earlier, when Jamie was pregnant with Bethany. Rich himself had designed the sprawling L-shaped rambler that overlooked Puget Sound, and he was justifiably proud.

"Yes, I need to borrow a suit," Jason muttered, not giving his brother the satisfaction of explaining. Already he regretted having volunteered to be a chaperone for this dance. No matter how hard he tried, he wasn't going to be whirling around a dance floor as if he knew what he was doing. He'd probably make a fool of himself in front of Charlotte and a bunch of smart-aleck ninth-graders.

As an engineer, Rich was required to

dress more formally on the job than Jason was. Jason owned a suit, but it was outdated. Maybe if he waited a few more years it would become fashionable again.

If the truth be known, he wasn't even sure when he'd last worn it. Sometime in college, he guessed. He'd buy another one if he thought he'd get any use out of it, but that didn't seem likely.

"What do you need a suit for?" Rich asked outright.

"I wouldn't be borrowing one if I'd known I was going to face an inquisition."

Rich chuckled, clearly enjoying Jason's discomfort. "I just want to be sure you aren't going to run off and marry Charlotte. Mom would kill you if you pulled a stunt like that."

Jason snickered, hoping to give the impression that marriage was the furthest thing from his mind, which it was. Wasn't it?

"Hey, don't act like it couldn't happen," Rich said, pushing hangers aside as he sorted through several tailored jackets. "With our family's history, it wouldn't be unheard-of for you to elope."

Jason couldn't argue with that. It had all started with Taylor. A few years back, his sister had moved to Montana and within three months had married Russ Palmer. The decision to marry had apparently been impulsive—and it happened while they were chaperoning the high-school drill team in Reno. The deed was done by the time they bothered to contact any family.

Jason frowned. Taylor had been a chaperone, too, and look where it had led. This high-school dance was beginning to sound more and more dangerous.

Christy had married on the sly, too, again without telling anyone in the family. There were extenuating circumstances in her case, however. Well, sort of. His youngest sister had actually been engaged—to a lawyer, James Wilkens—when she'd gone to Idaho with Cody Franklin and married him. Their marriage had caused quite a ruckus in the family, but eventually everything had been smoothed over. Anyway, Christy was much better suited to Cody than to James, although the attorney had remained a good family friend.

Rich had followed suit, marrying Jamie with some idiotic idea of being a sperm donor for her baby. Jason had stood up for his brother, but he'd known from the beginning that the two of them were in love. He'd predicted that this sperm donor business wouldn't pan out, and he'd been right. Jamie had gotten pregnant, sooner than either of them had expected, and the process hadn't involved any artificial insemination, either.

Paul had been next. Diane, Paul's first wife, had died tragically, shortly after giving birth to Kelsey. Her loss had sent the family reeling. For six months, Paul had shunned his family's offers of help, attempting to balance his duties at home with his job and at the same time comfort his grieving children, all preschoolers. He'd been proud and angry. Leah, Diane's sister, had convinced him he couldn't continue alone. She'd given up her teaching position at the college and moved in with Paul and the children. Shortly afterward, they were married. But once again, no one in the family was informed of the ceremony.

The only single Manning left was Jason, and he didn't plan to get married. He'd decided that years before. It was unfortunate that his parents had been cheated out of putting on a large wedding, but those were the breaks. He wasn't marching down any aisle just to satisfy his mother's need to work with caterers and some florist friend she'd known for years.

"So, Jase," Rich said casually, breaking into his thoughts. "How are things with you and Charlotte?"

"Fine."

"Fine?" Rich repeated, with that smug look Jason found so irritating.

"You don't need to concern yourself with my affairs," Jason said, resenting the way Rich and Paul made his love life their business.

"Are you going to ask her to marry you?" Almost in afterthought, Rich held up a well-cut gray suit coat. The tailoring was excellent and the material was top of the line.

Jason ignored the question and reached for the jacket, trying it on over his black T-shirt with *Seattle at Night* silk-screened across the front.

"What are your intentions toward Charlotte?" Rich asked with a pensive frown. He sounded oddly formal—and unusually serious.

"My intentions are my own, but since you asked," Jason said, turning around to admire his profile in the full-length mirror, "I'll tell you.... They're dishonorable, as always." He tried to make a joke of it, laugh off the attraction he'd been battling from the moment he'd met Charlotte Weston over a leaky faucet.

His joke, however, fell decidedly flat.

"Not this time, big brother."

"What do you mean by that?" Jason demanded. He didn't like his brother sticking his nose where it didn't belong, but he couldn't help being curious about Rich's remark.

"You're in love with her."

"Is that right?" Jason returned flippantly.

"It's the first time you've ever invited a woman to watch you play softball."

Rich made it sound as if that alone was enough to force him into a shotgun wedding. Jason refused to get into an argument with his younger brother. It wouldn't do him any good. Just because Rich and Jamie were so happy together, his brother seemed to think he was an expert on the subject of love and marriage. Jason didn't want to be the one to disillusion him.

Perhaps he did have some deep affection for Charlotte, Jason told himself. He'd be the first to admit he was strongly attracted to her, but marriage? Out of the question.

This was a familiar argument, one he'd worked through early in their relationship. It had worried him then, but he'd been so fascinated with her that he'd pushed his apprehensions to the back of his mind, deciding to take one day at a time.

He'd face one hurdle, he decided, before he confronted another. For now, the obstacle was their physical relationship. When she trusted him enough to put aside her fears and allow him to make love to her, it would be time to reevaluate what was happening between them. But not yet.

"Are you going to let me borrow the suit or not?" Jason asked stiffly. "If I have to stand here and listen to a lecture, too, I'd rather go to the rental shop."

He half expected Rich to jerk the coat off his shoulders and send him on his way. Instead, his youngest brother grinned, as if he knew something Jason didn't. It was another irritating habit of his.

"You're welcome to keep the suit as long as you like," Rich assured him. "You never know when you're suddenly going to need one."

Friday evening came, and it took Jason a full half hour to knot his tie correctly. He was out of practice, and getting it just right frus-

trated him. He should've borrowed the clip-
on variety, but he hadn't thought of asking for
one. No doubt Rich had plenty of each type.

Surveying his reflection in the mirror, he
barely recognized himself. He was tall, best-
ing his brothers by an inch or more, his shoulders were wide and, if he had anything to
be proud of physically, it was that his stomach had remained flat. Haphazard meals and
baseball did that for a man.

Charlotte probably wouldn't recognize
him, either. If memory served, it was the first
time she'd gone anywhere with him when he
wasn't wearing a baseball cap. He brushed
his hand along the side of his head, making
sure his hair stayed flat. He carefully examined himself to see if he could find any gray
hairs for a more distinguished look. When he
didn't, he was actually disappointed.

He checked his watch. If everything had
gone according to schedule, Carrie would
have been picked up fifteen minutes ago for a
pre-dance buffet. Since the dance didn't start
for another two hours, Jason had suggested
taking Charlotte out to dinner.

He didn't know what had gotten into him
lately. He'd made reservations at an expen-

sive restaurant, and ordered a fancy corsage to give her when they arrived.

Normally, his idea of a night on the town included pizza, beer and a Mariners' game. Drag an irresistible woman into his life, and before he knew it, he was forking out major bucks for dinner and flowers. The thing was, he'd come up with the idea on his own and was even excited about it, knowing how pleased Charlotte would be.

He'd seen this happen with his friends—his brothers, too—but he would never have believed *he'd* fall such willing prey to a woman's charms. It wouldn't have happened with anyone but Charlotte. Of that, he was certain.

At exactly seven, he walked over to Charlotte's apartment and rang the bell. She kept him waiting for several minutes before she opened the door—not a promising sign.

When she finally did come, Jason was about to complain. He was going to a lot of trouble for this blasted dance; the least she could do was be ready on time.

Whatever he'd intended to say, however, flew out of his mind when he saw Charlotte. For the longest moment of his life, he stood there immobile.

This was Charlotte! She was…stunning.

"I'm...sorry," she said, sounding flustered. "I didn't mean to keep you standing out here, but I'm having a problem with this dress."

She was beautiful.

The word didn't begin to describe how breathtaking she looked. Her hair was done in a way he'd never seen before, swirled to one side, exposing the smooth skin of her cheek and her long, slender neck. Dangling gold earrings swung from her ears. Her eyes were a brighter blue than ever before, the color of the sky washed clean by a summer squall. Her dress was a paler shade of blue... Her dress... Jason's gaze slid over the sleeveless dress with its tight bodice and flared skirt, and an invisible hand seemed to appear out of thin air and knock him senseless.

"Jason." Her eyes implored him as she held one hand behind her back. "Is something wrong? I look terrible, don't I? Don't worry about hurting my feelings... This dress is too fancy, isn't it?"

It was all he could do to close his mouth. "You look...fabulous." Which was the understatement of the century. Jason felt sorry that he wasn't more sophisticated and urbane.

If he had been, he might have told her how exquisite she was. He might have found the words to say he'd gladly rework the knot in his tie for another hour if it meant he could spend the evening with her. For the first time since he'd donned the suit jacket, he felt no remorse for volunteering to escort Charlotte to her daughter's dance.

"I can't get the zipper all the way up," Charlotte explained. "I was so busy helping Carrie get ready before Brad and his father arrived that I...I didn't get dressed myself, and now I can't reach the zipper. Would you mind?"

She presented him with her back and it was all Jason could do to pull the tab up instead of down. If he went on instinct he'd have had her out of that dress, in his arms and on the way to the bedroom. He couldn't recall a time he'd wanted a woman more than he did Charlotte Weston right then and there.

"Jason?" She glanced over her shoulder when he delayed.

His hand felt clammy, and at first his fingers refused to cooperate, but with some effort he managed to do as she asked, sliding the zipper up her back.

"Thank you," she said. "You can't imagine what a madhouse it's been around here," she went on. "Carrie was so nervous. She looked so grown-up. I can't believe my baby isn't a baby anymore."

Jason returned her smile. "My mother felt the same way when Christy—my sister—attended her first big dance."

Even now, Jason was having trouble forming coherent sentences.

"The dress isn't mine," she told him as she searched for her evening bag, wandering from one room to the next until she located it. "I borrowed it from one of my friends at the office… It's too close to the end of the month to go out and buy one." She sighed, sounding breathless. "Even if I'd had the extra money, I doubt I would've been able to find one at the last minute. I'd feel dreadful if something happened to Cheryl's dress."

"I borrowed the suit from my brother." Maintaining an intelligible conversation, he discovered, wasn't as much of a problem as keeping his eyes off her.

Charlotte drew in a deep, steadying breath. "I know it's silly, but I'm as nervous as Carrie."

He smiled, trying to reassure her.

"The last dance I attended was in college,"

she said. "I...I don't know if I can dance any-more."

"I'm not exactly light on my feet, Char-lotte," Jason felt obliged to remind her. He'd warned her earlier, but he doubted she'd taken him seriously.

"Do you think we should practice?" she asked.

She was gazing up at him with wide eyes. Jason would've given everything he owned to find out if she was feeling anything close to the emotional havoc he was.

"Practice?" he echoed. "That's an idea." He swallowed, wondering exactly what he was inviting. Trouble with a capital *T,* consider-ing the way his body was reacting.

Charlotte set aside her evening bag and walked into his embrace. "I'm afraid I'm not going to be very good at this," she murmured.

"Don't worry. Hey, as far as I'm concerned, those ninth-graders are going to dance circles around us anyway."

Charlotte's laugh sounded sweet and soft, and Jason's heart constricted. Could this be love? This pleasure he felt in doing small things for her—like the dinner and flowers?

This need to hold her in his arms? This desire to be with her and her alone?

The feel of Charlotte's body against his was the purest form of torture he'd ever experienced. She fit in his arms as though she belonged there. Had always belonged there. He tried to ignore how right it felt.

And couldn't.

He tried to ignore the fragrance of wildflowers that whispered through her hair whenever she moved her head.

And didn't.

He tried, but failed.

Everything went fairly well for the first few minutes. At least he wasn't stepping on her feet. Then Jason realized their feet weren't moving and they were staring at each other more than they were dancing. Gazing at each other with starry-eyed wonder.

He shifted his hand upward, wanting to lessen the feeling of intimacy, but his fingers inadvertently grazed the skin of her upper back.

Either he kissed her now or he'd regret it the rest of the night. Either he continued the pretense or confessed openly to how vulnerable she made him feel.

He brought her closer to him. He could feel

her heart racing, echoing his own. Once he kissed her, he knew there'd be no stopping. Not this time.

He lowered his head ever so slightly and waited.

Charlotte sighed, closed her eyes and lifted her mouth enticingly to his. He suspected she was unconscious of what she was doing, what she was seeking.

Frankly, Jason didn't care. He was so hungry for the taste of her, nothing mattered. His mouth found hers and he groaned. Charlotte did, too.

He hadn't touched her in days, wanting to give her time, give himself time to define the boundaries of their relationship. It had been too long. He felt so needy he trembled.

The kiss was long, slow, deliberate.

Slowly, reluctantly dragging his mouth from hers, he created a small distance between them. Her eyes slowly fluttered open and met his.

"Jason?"

"I want you, Charlotte." He couldn't be any plainer than that. "I need you."

Emotion flickered in her gaze. Was it fear? Pain? Jason found it impossible to tell.

"Do you want to stop?" His hands were

in her hair. By the time she lifted her mouth from his, Jason was melting with a need so powerful it throbbed within him.

Charlotte sighed into the hollow of his throat. "Jason, will you be angry with me?"

He saw the emotions assailing her, but noted the dignified way in which she tilted her chin and the proud squaring of her shoulders.

"No, I won't be angry."

She relaxed. Visibly. "Didn't you tell me you made dinner reservations for seven-thirty?"

"Yes." He recognized her fear and tried to ignore his own disappointment.

Self-conscious now, Charlotte broke away, quietly adjusting her clothes, then retrieved her evening bag. It wasn't until she looked up at him that he saw the anguish in her eyes.

He didn't know what her ex-husband—he assumed it was her ex-husband—had done. Her gaze linked with his, regret and misery so evident it was all he could do not to reach for her again. To comfort, not to kiss. To offer her solace, not passion.

Now, more than ever, Jason was determined to discover how her ex-husband had hurt her so badly. Determined to help her recover and teach her how beautiful love could be.

* * *

Charlotte was shaken to her very core. The intensity of their kisses had grown fervent and passionate, near the point of no return. If she'd given him the least bit of encouragement, he would have carried her into the bedroom.

For one wild moment, she'd been tempted to let him. Then the haze of desire had faded enough for sanity to return.

She felt grateful that Jason had allowed her to regain her senses, had given her the option to stop or proceed. Not like Tom…

Charlotte was jarred by this latest exchange even more than the other times Jason had held her and kissed her.

He'd almost made her forget.

Since her divorce, Charlotte had been content in her own small, secure world. The world she'd so carefully constructed for herself and Carrie. It had been the two of them, prevailing against all odds, forging a life together. The borders of her world had been narrow and confining, but Charlotte had made peace with that, had accepted its limitations.

Then a series of events had thrown her into confusion. It had all started at the baby shower for her friend Kathy Crenshaw. Charlotte had held the newborn in her arms and the longing she'd managed to ignore all these years had struck her full-force.

Shortly afterward she'd met Jason, and her life hadn't been the same since.

Because of Jason, she'd recognized how restricted her world had become. How limited. If that wasn't enough, he'd shown her glimpses of a life she'd never dared hope existed. He'd taught her to dream, to believe in the impossible.

Almost.

After a protracted farewell to Higgins, they went out to the parking lot. Jason opened the car door and helped her inside, then stood in the fresh air for several minutes, hands in his coat pockets. He closed his eyes and turned his face toward the night sky.

Charlotte knew it was difficult for a man to cut the lovemaking off as abruptly as they'd done. He needed a few minutes to compose himself.

She watched him as he climbed into the car. He hesitated after inserting the key into the ignition and smiled over at her. "Ready?"

Charlotte nodded. "Are you…all right?"

"Never finer," he assured her, then clasped her hand to kiss her knuckles.

Nine

Jason Manning was a romantic. Beneath that I-don't-give-a-damn attitude was a tenderness and warmth that left Charlotte feeling like a starry-eyed adolescent. The candlelight dinner at an elegant cliffside restaurant had been wonderful. There he'd given her a fragrant rosebud corsage that was so lovely, it had brought tears to her eyes.

The dance had been the best part of their evening. They'd had a delightful time, despite being surrounded by ninth-graders and forced to endure an earsplitting mixture of songs.

Jason and Charlotte had discovered early on that they weren't going to be able to dance to rap music. After a number of hilarious attempts, they'd given up. Several of their efforts had left Charlotte laughing so hard, her ribs ached.

Jason had been equally amused, and after their unsuccessful attempts to blend in with the kids, he'd reached for Charlotte, guiding her into his arms. She'd draped her wrists loosely around his neck and he placed his hands on her hips. Then they'd invented their own dance....

Although Charlotte knew Carrie had risked her "cool" status, her daughter had come to her, eyes bright with excitement, to confess it wasn't so bad having her mother chaperone a dance, after all.

After the dance, while Carrie and Brad attended the nearby party, Charlotte and Jason sat outside in the schoolyard, gazing at the stars, laughing and kissing. Not the passionate, soul-deep kisses of earlier, but tender, sweet ones. By the end of the evening the barriers surrounding her heart had started to crumble.

Charlotte and Carrie came home at a respectable hour, their heads filled with romance. With barely a word, they wandered off to bed, passing each other like sleepwalkers in the hall.

Several hours later, Charlotte, unable to sleep, wrapped her memories around her like a cloak. Not since her own schooldays had she been more at ease with a man. In the space of one evening, she'd come to realize—without doubt, fear or regret—that she was deeply in love with Jason Manning.

After an hour of savoring every moment, she found she could finally sleep, knowing she'd be with him the next morning when he picked her up for the game.

"You ready, Mom?" Carrie called happily from the kitchen. It was shortly after ten. "Jason'll be here any minute."

Charlotte sucked in her stomach and zipped up her skinny jeans. Then she reached for a clean sweatshirt and tossed it over her head. Jason was already in the kitchen, checking the contents of the picnic basket, when she sauntered in from her bedroom. Her heart did a little dance when she saw him.

"Good morning." She felt shy, and couldn't explain it.

He turned around and their eyes met before he sent her a wide smile. "'Morning."

Charlotte opened the refrigerator and withdrew a six-pack of diet soda to add to the cooler.

"Is that all I get—just a friendly 'good

morning'?" he asked, keeping his voice low so Carrie wouldn't hear.

"What else do you want?"

"You should know the answer to that. I swear, Charlotte, leaving you last night was one of the hardest things I've ever done." He slipped his arms around her waist and nuzzled his face in the slope of her neck.

Charlotte twisted around and stared up at him. "It was?"

"The only thing that got me through it was knowing I'd be with you again this morning." He lowered his mouth to hers, and she parted her lips. The kiss was slow and deep and hot.

"Honestly, you two are getting ridiculous," Carrie said from behind Charlotte. "Even Higgins thinks so." At the last minute, Carrie had convinced her they should bring the dog. Charlotte wasn't sure he was healed enough to run around the park, but Carrie had phoned Jason and he'd felt it would be all right.

"You ready?" Jason asked, picking up the wicker basket, his hand around Charlotte's waist as though, even now, it was difficult to let her go.

"*I've* been ready for the last ten minutes,"

Carrie said pointedly, holding Higgins's leash and leading him to Jason's car.

On the ride across town, Jason put on a CD and the three of them sang along with Bon Jovi. But as they pulled into the massive parking lot, Jason's voice stopped abruptly.

"What's wrong?" Charlotte asked.

"Nothing for you to worry about." He tried to reassure her with a smile, but she wasn't so easily fooled. She glanced around, wondering what could possibly be amiss. She couldn't imagine, unless it was a vehicle he happened to recognize.

"I'm going to take Higgins for a walk," Carrie announced as soon as she'd climbed out of the backseat. Charlotte knew her daughter was eager to show off the dog to Ryan, Ronnie and the other children.

When Jason was opening the trunk of his car and removing his softball equipment, Charlotte spoke.

"Is there someone here you'd rather I not meet? An old girlfriend, a former lover?"

He turned and his gaze met hers. He smiled, a smile that started with his eyes and worked its way down to his mouth. "Nothing quite so dramatic. My parents are here."

"I see," she said. "You'd rather I wasn't with you."

"No," he said vehemently, and she realized he wanted her with him as much as she wanted to be. A rugged sigh followed his response. "I don't like the idea of you having to endure another inquisition."

"I'm a big girl."

"You don't know my mother."

"I'd like to, though," Charlotte assured him. She couldn't help thinking Jason's parents must be exceptional people, to have raised such a wonderful family. Before meeting the Manning clan, she'd known so little of what it meant to be part of a family, one in which everyone supported and encouraged one another. Where joys were shared and grief divided. All her life, Charlotte had been on the outside looking in, yearning for that special bond.

"They're going to drive you crazy with questions," he said grimly.

"Don't worry about it. I know how to be evasive. You forget, I'm the mother of a teenage daughter."

Jason's laugh was automatic. He grinned over at her, tossed a baseball bat over one shoulder and reached for her hand, linking their fingers. Linking them in a way that would dissolve any doubts.

Charlotte's heart sang with a joy that radiated from her heart.

They strolled casually, hand in hand, across the freshly mowed lawn. Jason's steps slowed as they approached the playing field.

Charlotte glanced up to find his eyes on her. "I just pray I can keep from hitting a home run," he whispered.

Charlotte laughed as they walked toward the older couple talking with Paul and Rich. Jason made the introductions and Charlotte smiled warmly and held her hand out to his parents.

"I've been looking forward to meeting you," she said confidently. "After getting to know Jason and his brothers, I can't help thinking you two must be very special people."

Jason waited a restless twenty-four hours for the summons. It arrived Sunday morning, disguised as an invitation to dinner at his parents' house that same evening. Jason, however, wasn't fooled. His mother intended to feed him, but he knew he'd be obliged to sing for his supper.

He showed up promptly at six and was pleased to see that his mother had gone to the trouble of preparing all his favorites. Homemade rolls hot from the oven. Crispy fried chicken, mashed potatoes and gravy, fresh-picked peas. A molded gelatin salad rested in the center of the dining-room table.

Jason had always been a meat-and-potatoes man, unless he had to cook for himself, which unfortunately he did most evenings. His eating habits were atrocious and he knew it. A homemade dinner like this was a rare treat.

"We don't see nearly enough of you," his mother said, as the three of them sat down at the table.

Jason noted that she'd set out her best china and silverware, as well as linen napkins and a matching tablecloth. This was going to be a heavy-duty interrogation. And it didn't look as if he had much chance of escaping before his mother ferreted out the information she wanted.

His father handed him the platter of chicken and Jason thought he might have read sympathy in his eyes.

"Generally, when your brothers are here for dinner, I get so involved with the grandchildren," his mother said conversationally. "You and I don't have much of a chance to talk."

"We talk," Jason said, reaching for the rolls and adding three to his plate, along with a thick slab of butter and a spoonful of strawberry preserves. His mother would have to wait for her information while he enjoyed his dinner.

"Gravy, son?"

"Thanks, Dad." A look of understanding passed between them.

"I hardly know what's going on in your life these days," his mother continued, undaunted. "I haven't seen you in a month of Sundays."

"That's not true, Elizabeth. Jason was over two weeks ago. Now, let the boy eat. You can drill him about Charlotte later."

His father was nothing if not direct. His mother didn't even pretend to be affronted; she simply sighed and nodded. "If you insist."

"I do," his father muttered, ladling gravy over a modest pile of mashed potatoes. He set the gravy boat aside and shook his head. "I don't understand you, Elizabeth. You've been half starving me for months, claiming we've got to start eating healthier. I've been eating salads and fish and broiled chicken. Now *this*.

I'm beginning to feel like it's my last dinner before facing the executioner."

"This is Jason's favorite dinner!" Elizabeth declared righteously.

"Don't be fooled, son," Eric Manning said, his elbows on the table. "Your mother's after something big this time."

"Eric!"

"Sorry, dear," Jason's father said contritely, then winked at him.

If his mouth hadn't been full of homemade bread, Jason would have laughed. His mother was in quite a mood. His father, too, but he was well aware of the love they shared. They had the kind of relationship he'd always hoped to have with a woman himself. For the first time in his life, he felt that might be possible.

They ate in relative silence with short discourses from Jason as he answered their questions about the veterinary hospital and his practice. He noticed how carefully his mother steered away from the subject of Charlotte and his social life.

No sooner had Jason and his father cleared the table than his mother brought out a deep-dish apple pie. Even the dessert was Jason's favorite.

While she dished up heaping bowlfuls and added ice cream, his father poured coffee.

"Now, Eric?" she asked, looking expectantly toward her husband.

"If you insist."

Jason glanced from his mother to his father, realizing his reprieve was about to end.

"I most certainly do. Jason," she said, shifting her attention to him, "as you probably know, your father and I are curious about you and Charlotte. *Very* curious."

"Yeah, I had that impression."

"We both liked her very much."

"She's a likable person," Jason said.

"How'd you meet her?"

He finished his pie, tipping the bowl on its side and spooning up the last of the melted ice cream. When he was convinced he'd gotten every drop, he wiped his mouth with the napkin, set it aside and reached for his coffee.

"She lives in the apartment complex."

"Widowed?"

"Divorced." He wasn't going to volunteer any more information than necessary.

"Are you in love with her?"

His mother was going for the jugular. Jason supposed she was entitled to the truth, since she'd gone to so much trouble with this dinner.

"Yes." The reaction he received was definitely satisfying. His mother's eyes grew huge, and she glanced excitedly at his father.

"I thought as much," she murmured.

"It's obvious the boy's in love, Elizabeth. I told you so, didn't I?"

"But it makes all the difference in the world that he's willing to admit it himself."

"Charlotte means a lot to me," Jason added without hesitation.

"Are you going to marry her?" His mother's voice had a breathless, hopeful quality.

Jason sipped his coffee. He was in love with Charlotte, no question. He woke in the morning and his first thoughts were of her. When he went to bed at night, she was there in his mind, following him into sleep. His whole day was focused on when he'd see her again. Kiss her again.

"Jason?" his mother urged.

"Yes, I'm sure I'll eventually marry Charlotte."

"Hot damn." His father slapped the table.

"Oh, Jason, I couldn't be happier." His mother dabbed the corners of her eyes with a napkin. "I'm so pleased," she said with a sniffle, reaching for her husband's hand.

"I'm happy you two are so happy." Jason hadn't talked about marriage with Charlotte yet, but he'd do that in due course. They were still beginning to know each other, feel comfortable together. By next summer at just about this time, they'd be ready to take such a monumental step.

"Now this is important, son," his father said, his eyes serious. "Your mother and I want your word that you're not going to do what your sisters and Rich and Paul did. In other words, don't marry Charlotte without the family being there."

Elizabeth backed her husband up. "I've waited all these years for a family wedding and I refuse to be cheated out of my last chance. Do you understand me, Jason?"

"Don't worry," Jason said calmly. "When Charlotte and I get married, we'll do it up big, just for you. The whole nine yards."

"A reception, with a dinner and dance?" His mother's eyes implored him.

"As long as Charlotte agrees, and I'm sure she will. She enjoys that sort of thing."

"But will she mind…my helping with the arrangements?"

Jason shrugged. "My guess is she'd welcome it. She doesn't have any family of her own, you know."

"Personally, I don't care if your mother has her hand in the arrangements or not," his father muttered. "I just want to be sure you aren't going to marry Charlotte behind our backs."

"I already promised I wouldn't." Still, given their family's history, Jason could understand his parents' skepticism.

"So I have your word on this?" his mother asked anxiously.

"My word of honor. Only..."

"Only what?" His mother looked concerned.

"Nothing, Mom. Don't worry about it."

"What is it?" she demanded.

"Well, I was wondering... Once Charlotte and I decide to marry, would you show her how to make fried chicken like yours?"

It wasn't fair to bother Jason with her problems, but there wasn't anyone she trusted more, anyone's opinion she valued as much. Her day at the office had been one of the worst ever. Her boss, Mr. Ward, had been unreasonable and demanding in the past, but his abuse that afternoon had reached an all-time high. He'd shouted at her, called her incompetent, belittled her. And it had been over something that was completely out of her control. A client had left the agency due to a problem with accounting, not anything Charlotte had done, yet she'd taken the brunt of Mr. Ward's anger. Unfortunately the insurance agency wasn't large enough to have a Human Resources department, so there was no one to complain to, no recourse to speak of.

It wasn't the first time and it wouldn't be the last. For three years she'd been employed as an executive assistant at the insurance agency. In the beginning she'd enjoyed her job and thrived on the challenge. Then, six months ago, Mr. Beatty, her original boss, had retired, and she'd found his replacement to be the worst kind of supervisor.

She'd made her decision earlier that afternoon, prepared her letter of resignation and placed it on Mr. Ward's desk before leaving the office. Although she'd felt confident when she left work, she was vacillating now, uncertain that she'd made the right decision.

It always seemed to be like this. She'd become indignant, decide to leave, and later, after her anger had cooled, she'd change her mind. Mr. Ward would seem repentant, try to convince her that his outbursts weren't personal; they were just his way. She'd start to believe him, at least until the next time.

Then it occurred to her.

What kind of woman would allow a man to verbally abuse her like that? What kind of woman allowed herself to be swayed by cheap talk and empty promises? The kind of woman who'd stayed married to Tom Weston for as long as she had, that was who.

She needed a sounding board, someone who'd listen to her frustration and doubts without casting judgment, without anger. Someone whose self-esteem was strong enough to accept her decisions whether she took his advice or not. Someone like Jason Manning.

Jason answered the phone immediately, sounding delighted to hear from her.

"I...I had a crummy day," she said when he asked. "Do you...would you go for a walk with me?" She considered bringing Higgins, but he was curled up with Carrie on the sofa.

"I'll be right over."

As Charlotte left, Carrie was talking on the phone with Brad. She hadn't told her daughter about quitting her job, although she was sure Carrie would cheer her decision.

"Hello," Jason said, kissing her lightly on the lips when she stepped out the door.

Charlotte closed her eyes. They joined hands and walked in the direction of the community park several blocks over.

The evening was beautiful. The fragrance of rhododendrons filled the evening air, mingling with the scent of blooming azaleas. Birds chirped and several people were getting a start on their yard work.

"I…did something I'm not positive I should have done," she said, keeping her eyes lowered.

"Was it illegal?"

The question made her smile. "No."

"Then why look so grave?"

"Well…"

"Do you want to tell me about it?"

She nodded, grateful they'd arrived at the park. Jason steered her toward an unoccupied bench and they sat down, his hand still holding hers.

"I…I don't get along with my boss. I'm good at my job—at least I used to be. But now… Mr. Ward makes unreasonable demands and takes out his frustration on whoever's close at hand. Unfortunately most of the time that's me."

"It doesn't seem like a healthy atmosphere to be working in."

"It isn't." Charlotte wasn't the only employee who felt unhappy. Cheryl was on the verge of giving her notice, too, and so were a couple of the others. It wouldn't surprise Charlotte if half the office staff left with her.

"Then you should quit."

He made it sound so straightforward.

"I've never been a quitter. It's one of the reasons the divorce was so difficult for me. I—" She stopped abruptly. She hadn't meant to drag her marriage into this, lay it out for Jason to examine…yet, perhaps it was time.

"Go on," he urged.

Charlotte inhaled deeply, gathering her resolve. "I wrote my two-weeks' notice this afternoon and left it on Mr. Ward's desk and now…now I'm having second thoughts."

"Why? Do you want to continue working at the agency?"

"No."

"Are you afraid you won't be able to find another job?"

"Not particularly—there's always a high demand for executive assistants. It's just…I know what's going to happen in the morning. Mr. Ward will arrive and read my letter and call me into his office. He'll apologize the way he always does. He seems to know exactly what to say, and when he's through with the apology, he'll offer me a token raise."

"It'd be nice if he threw in a bouquet of flowers."

"He might. He has before."

"Are you going to be swayed by that?"

"No-o." Her voice trembled and she shut her eyes to hold back the tears that burned. "It's so much like my marriage."

"Having to deal with an angry unreasonable man?"

"Yes…but more than that. Mr. Ward treats me the same way Tom did, and I swore… I promised myself I'd never allow another human being to do the things he did to me. And yet I take it, day after day, and I hate myself for it."

Jason's arm was around her now, hugging her close as if he wanted to absorb her pain. She was thankful he wasn't kissing her; she couldn't have endured that just then.

"I feel so angry when I let someone manipulate me. I want so badly to believe that things will change…that they'll get better. But they never do. Sooner or later Mr. Ward will go back to doing exactly what he's always done…

and I'll realize I've let myself be controlled again. I can't seem to deal with the truth.... I guess it's easier to deny everything than face the reality. Why is truth so painful?"

Jason waited a few minutes, his arm about her calm and comforting. "Is it your boss you're talking about or your ex-husband?"

"Both." Charlotte raised her head and wiped the tears from her eyes before they had a chance to fall. "Tom...had an affair. I knew it for months but...I pretended I didn't. I made believe we were happy and in love, while doing everything I could to win him back. But it wasn't enough... Now I know nothing would have been enough."

Jason didn't interrupt her with questions, once again she was grateful. The effort not to weep had produced a lump in her throat, and talking was almost painful. She hesitated, head still lowered.

Jason's mouth brushed her hair. "Your husband was a fool, Charlotte."

She didn't respond; she couldn't. Jason didn't know the full story, didn't understand that there'd been a reason Tom had turned to another woman. Any healthy male would have, or so her ex-husband had vehemently assured her time and again.

"I'm stubborn and hardheaded," she said, her voice cracking. "I don't know when to let go and…so I hold on, no matter how painful…or damaging."

"I can't tell you what to do," Jason said after a thoughtful moment, "but don't judge yourself so harshly. Some people know exactly what to say to get what they want. Everyone needs to hear they're important, that they're loved and appreciated. But those are only words, and talk is cheap. You got out of your marriage at the right time and—"

"No," she sobbed, "I didn't…. I didn't *want* out of the marriage, don't you see? It was Tom who asked for the divorce, Tom who forced everything into the open. I would've gone on pretending forever if he hadn't. I won't do it again. I won't! I'm quitting my job, Jason. I'm walking out two weeks from now and I won't look back. I swear to you, I won't look back."

There was a message from his mother when he returned to his apartment. His mind was heavy with everything he'd learned about Charlotte's marriage and he contemplated waiting to return his mother's call, but she'd sounded so excited.

Sighing, he reached for the phone. His mother answered on the first ring.

"Jason, I'm so glad you called! I have so much to tell you. I talked to Taylor and Christy and they've both agreed to come."

"Come?"

"You can't imagine what a day I've had," his mother continued, her voice animated. "I called Barbara Johnson, you remember Barbara, my friend who owns the floral shop, don't you? We went to high school together a thousand years ago."

"Mom…"

"Let me finish." With barely a pause to breathe, she went on, "Barbara was the one who got things started. She suggested we contact the yacht club right away and book a date for the reception. They're booked at least a year in advance. A year, I told myself. I know you, Jason, and when you're ready to do something, you don't want to wait an entire year. Barbara was right. The earliest date was August the year after next. I can tell you, I was shocked. I had no idea we'd need to book the reception so early."

"Reception? What reception?" Jason was starting to get a frightening premonition.

His mother ignored his question. "That's

when I learned there'd been a cancellation in July. This July! I couldn't believe our luck. Naturally I booked it that very instant. Then I contacted the caterers and, as luck would have it, they agreed to do the dinner, although it's only three weeks' notice. *Three weeks,* Jason. Three weeks. It sounds crazy to even attempt something of this magnitude, but we're going to pull it off without a hitch."

Jason's vague premonition was beginning to solidify. "Mom, what are you talking about?" he asked with growing anxiety.

Once again his mother disregarded his question. "That's when I phoned Taylor and Christy. They both called back to say they're coming. They've already made their plane reservations. Russ is coming, and Mandy, too. Remember Mandy, Russ's sister? She's in college now, you know."

"Coming? To *what,* Mother?" Jason demanded.

"Why, Jason, I've spent the day making the arrangements for your wedding to Charlotte. What else would I be talking about, for heaven's sake?"

Ten

"Mother, have you gone stark, raving mad?" Jason had difficulty keeping a rein on his anger. "How can you set a wedding date and hire caterers when I haven't even *mentioned* it to Charlotte? This is insane." He rubbed his face, wondering if he'd imagined this entire fiasco.

"Your father warned me you'd be angry, but, Jason, I know you. Once you and Charlotte decide to marry, you won't want to wait two years."

"Mom, I don't suppose it dawned on you that there are other places we could have a wedding reception—*if* we were actually having one. The yacht club isn't the only venue in this town."

"Frankly, no, it didn't occur to me," his mother returned calmly. "Since we're just going to have one formal wedding in this family, we're doing it up big, and the yacht club's the best alternative."

Jason could see he was losing ground. "Let me talk to Dad."

"But, Jason—"

"Mother!"

"All right, just a minute."

That minute seemed to take an hour. By the time he had his father on the line, Jason was as angry as he'd ever been. The instant he heard Eric pick up the receiver, he shouted, "Has Mother gone crazy? Have you? How could you let things go this far?"

His father chuckled, apparently amused, something Jason most definitely wasn't. "I agree with you," his father said breezily, "your mother has gone a little crazy."

"Dad, listen, I know you and Mom mean well, but I refuse to let you run my life. Scheduling the reception, talking to florists, I can't believe you'd allow Mom to do all this without talking to me first."

"Don't forget, she's involved Taylor and Christy, as well. That's when I thought she'd stepped over the line. You haven't even asked Charlotte to marry you, and Elizabeth's got your sisters choosing bridesmaids' dresses.

By the way, I don't suppose she told you about the honeymoon? Two weeks in Hawaii—it's our wedding gift to you."

Jason clenched his fist at his side and closed his eyes, trying to calm himself. It didn't work. The situation was absurd. And he was beginning to see that his father was in on this nonsense. "Two weeks in Hawaii... Taylor and Christy choosing bridesmaids' dresses. You've both gone off the deep end."

"To your mother's credit, she didn't intend for this to happen. It just did. I know you're upset now, and to be honest, I don't blame you, but once you get used to the idea, it doesn't sound so ludicrous."

Get used to the idea, Jason mused. He felt like he was in the middle of a nightmare. "You honestly think I should agree to this... this outrageousness?" He could barely speak.

"Answer me this. Are you in love with Charlotte?"

"Yes." That much was a given— he'd already told his parents so.

"Do you intend to ask her to marry you?"

His dad knew the answer to that, too. "Yes...eventually, in my own time and my own way."

"If you're planning to marry the girl anyway, then what's the problem?"

"I wasn't going to do it in three weeks!"

"Three weeks, three months, what's the difference?"

Jason couldn't believe it. His father was talking pure craziness.

"I realize your mother and I went about this wrong, but after what happened with your brothers and sisters, all I ask is that you cut us a little slack."

"A little slack," he snorted. "Marriage is a serious step. A man doesn't make that kind of decision one minute and march up the aisle the next."

"I used to feel that way myself, but it's pretty much what happened with Taylor and Russ, as well as Christy and Cody. They made up their minds, then went right ahead and did it."

"All right, all right," Jason muttered, willing to concede the point. Their weddings were spontaneous, to say the least. Same for Rich and Paul.

"I agree, marriage is a serious step," his father went on calmly, "but if you're in love with Charlotte and intend to marry her anyway, I don't see the harm in your mother getting the ball rolling."

The ball rolling. She'd started an avalanche. "Don't you think Mom's just a tad premature?"

"Perhaps," his father agreed amicably enough. "But you can't really blame her for that. She got caught up in the excitement of the moment. Once she talked to the yacht club, everything sort of fell into place. It makes sense once you analyze it. You've been a bachelor a long time, Jason. If you're as serious about marrying Charlotte as you claim, my advice is, just do it. If you wait, you might talk yourself out of it."

"Do it," Jason echoed. "You make marriage sound like taking up an exercise program." He could see he wasn't going to make any more headway with his father than he had his mother.

"Think about it, all right? That's all I ask."

"Aren't you forgetting something?"

"What?"

"Charlotte might say no."

His father laughed. "Charlotte's as much in love with you as you are with her. She'll marry you in a New York minute and we both know it."

"But, Dad…"

"Just think about it overnight. That's all your mother and I are asking. If you decide you'd rather not go through with this, then phone us in the morning and we'll put a stop to everything."

"I don't need to sleep on this," Jason argued. "I can tell you right now that I'm not going to agree. I've never heard anything more absurd in my life. A wedding in a few weeks! I was thinking more along the lines of two or three years!"

A heavy silence followed his words. "Then you must not be as much in love as your mother and I assumed. Give us a call in the morning," his father said and hung up the phone.

Jason was too furious to stand still. He paced his living room, jerked his baseball cap off his head and slapped it against his thigh. He tried to smooth out the crease in the bill, realized he couldn't and tossed the hat on top of the television.

Earlier that evening, he'd been talking to Charlotte about this very thing—people manipulating and controlling others. Well, he wasn't about to fall prey to it now. Especially not with his parents.

If he allowed his mother to schedule his wedding, there was no telling where she'd stop. The next thing he knew she'd be meddling in *all* his personal affairs. She'd be deciding when it was time for him and Charlotte to have a family.

He drew in a deep, calming breath to clear his head.

His assessment of his mother was unfair, he told himself a few minutes later. His parents hadn't interfered in his brothers' or sisters' marriages. From what he understood, they'd suggested Leah and Paul get married, but that was common sense. Leah and Paul should have seen it themselves. He knew his parents had debated long and hard about confronting them and had done so reluctantly, after much soul-searching.

But arranging his marriage to Charlotte was an entirely different matter. They'd stepped over the boundary there—although… although he did understand how easy it must have been to get caught up in the heat of the moment. Getting the date at the yacht club had set everything in motion, and before either of his parents were aware of it, they'd planned the whole wedding.

As he recalled from his dinner conversation the day before, Jason had told his mother that Charlotte would welcome her assistance in planning the wedding. She'd done a bit more than suggest what type of flowers to use in the bridal bouquet, however.

No, it was out of the question.

Jason flatly refused to be a pawn. When he was ready to marry Charlotte he'd...

Married. He and Charlotte.

He needed at least a year just to get used to the idea. A man his age didn't surrender his freedom without plenty of serious thought.

Then he remembered the phenomenon of holding Charlotte in his arms, of loving her, and the simple pleasure he found in spending time with her. He tried to imagine what his life would be like without her and discovered he couldn't. So his belief that he wasn't ready flew out the window.

But marriage, he told himself, would take away his freedom. He'd never watch another game on TV again without feeling guilty—a wife would make sure of that. Women nagged and controlled, didn't they?

Charlotte was a woman, but she wasn't like the others he'd known. She'd been controlled and manipulated herself; she'd fought against it. Jason couldn't in all honesty believe she'd try the same tactics on him.

Once again his argument wouldn't hold.

All right, maybe there were more things to consider besides his freedom. But here, too, he was losing ground. He'd found freedom in Charlotte, freedom to be himself, freedom to look toward the future.

Charlotte wanted children.

Another contentious issue. Children. Carrie had said as much the day she'd stopped by his office to bribe him to take out her mother. If he married Charlotte, he might as well accept that a year or so down the road they'd have a baby.

So? Wasn't that what he wanted?

He hadn't thought much about a family until recently. He vividly remembered the sensations that had overwhelmed him the first time he'd seen Charlotte holding Jeremy. Watching her play with his brother's son had left him breathless. Of course, being hit by a fast-moving Frisbee might have contributed to that.

Okay, so he wanted children. A man didn't marry a woman without giving the prospect some consideration. Since he was well past thirty, and fast approaching forty, he should start thinking along those lines soon. Charlotte was nearly thirty-six herself, and he knew it was safer for a woman to give birth before the age of forty.

Which meant he had to throw out his idea of waiting two or three years to get married. If he was serious, and he was, they should do it soon.

But three weeks was *too* soon....

He'd sleep on it, Jason decided, take his father's advice and give this whole wedding business some thought. But he could say right now, that on general principles alone, he was against it.

An hour later, after tossing and turning and wreaking havoc with his bedsheets, Jason knew. Knew it from the way he couldn't keep his hands from clenching. Knew it from the way his stomach tensed.

He was going to marry Charlotte Weston. The wedding was already scheduled.

Charlotte didn't know what was wrong with him. Jason had fidgeted all through dinner, although dinner had been his idea. He'd called her early that morning, before she'd left for work, and invited her out.

The invitation had sounded offhand, spur

of the moment. Or that was how he'd apparently intended it to sound. But Charlotte wasn't fooled. His voice had tensed as though he wasn't sure she'd say yes—which was ridiculous. Surely he knew how crazy she was about him. Yet, when she assured him she'd be happy to join him for dinner, he hadn't seemed the least bit relieved.

She'd suggested Mr. Tamales, but he'd disagreed. Instead he'd chosen a fancy seafood restaurant near the harbor. She'd been looking forward to chicken enchiladas, but certainly wasn't disappointed with her shrimp Louis.

Charlotte could have sworn, however, that Jason hadn't eaten more than three bites of his wine-sautéed scallops. "Jason," she said after a long silence. "Is something bothering you?"

"No," he replied abruptly.

"You haven't said a word in the last five minutes. Aren't you feeling well?"

"My stomach's in knots." His reply was quick and short-tempered. He reached for his water glass, emptying ice chips into his mouth, then chewed on them fiercely.

"Do you want to leave?"

His eyes met hers and for an all-too-brief moment the tension eased from around his mouth. "Not yet."

"Okay," she said, wondering at his strange mood.

"How did everything go with your boss?" he asked, seeming to want to change the subject.

She'd already told him, but apparently he hadn't been paying attention. "He's angry, especially since two other people also gave their notice when they learned I wasn't changing my mind."

"Did he try to make staying worth your while?"

Charlotte nodded. "He offered me and the others a raise." Mr. Ward had called all three of them into his office, smugly claimed he was willing to overlook this small mutiny and offered them each a raise if they'd withdraw their resignations.

"You didn't take his bride—I mean bribe—did you?"

"No." Charlotte was still basking in the satisfaction she'd felt when she told Mr. Ward she wasn't interested in withdrawing her notice. Cheryl and Janice hadn't changed their minds, either. Mr. Ward had been stunned, but she knew that would soon pass.

Before the end of the two weeks, he'd try every manipulative tactic in the book. When she didn't give in, he'd try anger, his least effective tool.

She was through with a boss who was so angry and unreasonable. Through with guilt and regret and abuse. She already had a line on another job, although she would've enjoyed taking the summer off.

Unfortunately, she couldn't afford it. As it was, she only had two months' budget in her savings account, and it had taken her a year to accumulate that much. She called it her "attitude money." It was a whole lot easier to walk away from her position at the agency, knowing she had some cash to fall back on if she didn't get a job right away.

"How about dessert?" Jason suggested after the waitress had taken their dinner dishes away.

She shook her head. "No, thanks. I'm stuffed."

He looked disappointed at her response.

"You go ahead, though," she urged.

Jason immediately rejected the idea, proving her initial impression wrong. But if he *wasn't* craving dessert, what did he want? He seemed restless, yet obviously wasn't inclined to leave.

Whatever was bothering Jason wasn't trivial, Charlotte realized. Jason Manning wasn't a man easily unnerved. She wondered if it was something she'd done, something she'd said. She didn't know what to make of his behavior. Throughout dinner, she'd considered various explanations, none of which seemed all that logical.

The silence between them lingered as they sipped their after-dinner coffee. From the moment he'd picked her up, she'd been surprised that Jason was wearing a suit, the same attractive gray one he'd had on the night of the dance. His brother's suit. She knew very well that he didn't dress formally unless it was some important occasion. His entire wardrobe consisted of jeans and T-shirts.

He hated wearing a suit. Five minutes after they'd arrived at the dance, he'd loosened his tie, and had completely discarded it by the end of the evening. Why he'd worn one this evening remained a mystery.

Charlotte frowned, trying to analyze what was wrong. Waiting for Jason to tell her was making her nervous. He looked miserable, which made *her* increasingly miserable.

She felt close to Jason, closer than she'd felt to any man since Tom. She hadn't meant that to happen, and she didn't think Jason had, either. Their relationship had grown steadily more intense in the past weeks. She'd fallen in love—it was that simple—and thought he had, too.

But perhaps falling in love wasn't what Jason wanted. Perhaps he was trying to find a way to tell her they were in too deep, that he wanted out.

It made sense.

The fancy dinner, the hesitation and even regret. The fact that his eyes kept avoiding hers. The silence. That was the worst. The awkward silence, as though he couldn't bear to speak those final words.

"I'm ready to leave, if you are," she said with false enthusiasm.

He looked over at her, his expression uncertain. Perhaps he planned to tell her in the restaurant, in order to avoid a scene. She'd heard that was a popular tactic. All Charlotte wanted to do was leave, before she made a fool of herself by breaking into tears.

He was going to break up with her; she was sure of it. A hundred explanations crowded her mind. They'd gotten too close, too fast. It wasn't as if she was...unencumbered. True, she was single, but she had a child, and if a man was going to get serious with a woman, he'd prefer that she didn't bring along excess baggage. That was common knowledge. She'd heard it often enough from friends and acquaintances.

Jason's parents might have disapproved of her, too. It wasn't as if she came from a fine, upstanding family. His mother had asked her a number of questions Saturday morning about her parents and grandparents. Charlotte had found it difficult to explain that she had no idea where her father was, or even if he was still alive. Neither of the elder Mannings had seemed to disapprove of her openly. If anything, they'd been warm and gracious. But although they might have accepted her, even liked her, they might also think she was the wrong kind of woman for their son.

Jason paid the bill while Charlotte excused herself for a visit to the ladies' room, hoping to regain her composure.

He was waiting for her by the door when she returned.

Silence accompanied them into the parking lot.

Jason opened her door. By the time he'd walked around the front of his car, Charlotte's hold on her poise was tenuous. When he glanced in her direction, though, she managed a smile. Her pride demanded it.

Charlotte expected Jason to drive her directly to the apartment, since he hadn't been able to break the news to her at the restaurant. At least when he delivered the blow, it would be in the comfort of familiar surroundings.

But he drove to a deserted stretch of beach, then pulled off the road, climbed out of the car and came around to her side.

"It's late," she said, frowning at her watch. "I should be getting home. Carrie's by herself."

"In a minute." He wore a pensive frown, the same expression she'd seen all evening.

She gazed past him to the shoreline. Small breakers rolled onto the sand, their motion soothing. Charlotte wasn't soothed, however, and she looked away to the wide expanse of darkening sky. The scent of the sea hung in the air.

"Just say it," she muttered. Her patience had evaporated and she couldn't bear the painful silence anymore.

"You know?"

"Of course I know." She walked onto the sand, removed her shoes and purposefully forged ahead, stopping at a thick log that was charred at one end.

Swallowing a mouthful of self-pity, she looked over her shoulder to discover that Jason had followed her onto the beach. She almost wished he'd driven away, left her behind. It would've been easier that way.

Her legs didn't feel as if they'd support her much longer, so she sat on the log and stared sightlessly out at the horizon, waiting for him to begin his litany of excuses and stumbling explanations.

"Charlotte...I'm not very good at this sort of thing."

"Who is? Listen, it's been great." She strove to sound flippant and knew she'd failed. She lowered her gaze to her hands, forcing herself to continue. "I'll always be grateful for this time with you." Tears rolled down her cheeks and she brushed them aside, not daring to look at Jason. "But as we both know, all good things must come to an end...."

Jason said nothing. Not one word, and that made everything even more difficult.

His hands were buried in his pants pockets and when she glanced up at his face, she saw that his jaw was tightly clenched. She didn't understand his anger, not when she'd made it so easy for him.

"So you had me sit through that whole miserable dinner," he said with barely controlled antagonism. "Did you enjoy watching me squirm?"

"No."

"You know, Charlotte, if you weren't interested in marrying me in the first place you could have—"

"Marrying you!" Charlotte's head snapped up. "You planned on asking me to *marry* you?" For one wild second she was paralyzed with shock, unable to move or think. There must've been a mistake. It was a joke. Jason Manning was a confirmed bachelor, wasn't he? Despite her feelings for him, Charlotte had accepted that.

"Don't pretend you didn't know," he said.

"But I thought…I thought you wanted to stop seeing me."

He snickered as though he didn't believe her and turned away. "Why would I take you to a fancy restaurant if I wanted to say something as ridiculous as that?" He turned back, glaring at her.

"To let me down easy. What did you expect me to think, when you were in such a bad mood?"

"I already told you I'm no good at this sort of thing. If you want romance and a bunch of pretty words, you're going to have to marry someone else."

She was on her feet and not quite sure how she got there. "You honestly want to marry me?" she repeated as her eyes brimmed with tears. They were tears of relief. Tears of joy.

"Sit down," he said gruffly. "If I'm going to do this, I want to do it right."

Charlotte complied and was shocked when Jason got down on one knee directly in front of her. He cleared his throat. "I love you, Charlotte. I wasn't planning to fall in love with you, but I knew it was happening, and I let it happen because—well, I don't really know. It happened and I'm glad it did. I can't think of spending a day without you at my side. I can't imagine playing softball without you there. I love you. I love the chocolate chip cookies you bake. I admire you for the wonderful job you've done raising Carrie. I'm deeply impressed by your wisdom and courage."

"Oh, Jase." She blinked back her tears and brought her fingertips to her lips.

"You're the first woman I ever dated who let me be myself. You didn't feel obligated to clean up after me. You don't act as if my refrigerator's some kind of scary science experiment." He grinned, apparently pleased with his own wit. "You even like sports."

The lump in her throat made it impossible to speak. Tears ran unrestrained down her face. With all her heart she wanted to shout, "Yes, I'll marry you," and throw her arms around him. But she was afraid to believe Jason would continue to love her once he learned how inadequate she was, how worthless she was as a lover. She didn't know if she could bear to disappoint him.

"If it helps," he said in a low voice, "I talked to Carrie, and she's all for us getting married."

Charlotte sniffed tearfully. "You mean my daughter's given you her seal of approval?"

"Yup."

There was another silence. Then he said, "I don't mean to rush you, but I have this sore knee. I slid into first base last week and I've been in pain ever since. So, if you don't mind, I'd prefer a quick answer."

Before she could stop herself, before she could listen to her head instead of her heart, she nodded. It wasn't a very enthusiastic nod, perhaps, but Jason didn't seem to have any objections.

"Thank God," he murmured, awkwardly rising to his feet.

"You idiot. You didn't have to get down on your knee," she whispered through her tears.

"Yes, I did," he said, but he sounded grateful to be off it as he sat down on the log beside her. A deep sigh rumbled through his chest. "It wasn't the most romantic proposal, was it?"

"Oh, Jase, it was perfect," she said, touching the side of his face and gazing into his eyes. Her throat was tight and constricted. "What you said about not being able to live without me…that's how I feel about you. Sharing cookies, going to ball games, walking the dog together—it all sounds wonderful. I guess I'm not much of a romantic, either," she said with a shy laugh.

"I didn't buy a diamond ring. I figured you'd want to pick a setting yourself."

A ring. Charlotte froze. Soon he'd want to discuss a wedding date. A chill worked its way through her, the same cold feeling she'd experienced whenever Tom wanted to make love. A sick sensation would build in the pit of her stomach and by the time they went to bed she'd feel encased in ice. All Tom had to do was kiss her and he'd know. Then the tirades would begin, the accusations, the ugliness.

Jason was going to kiss her, too. Now. His lips grazed hers. Briefly. Lightly. The cold fear melted as if it had never been. Charlotte groaned and slipped her arms around his neck.

He kissed her again, but this time the kiss blossomed into something wild and erotic that left Charlotte panting, seeking more.

They drew apart, and she rested her forehead against his. When he spoke, his voice was husky and warm, as warm as heated brandy and just as intoxicating.

"We're going to be very good in bed," he whispered.

Charlotte tensed, panic a heartbeat away, but she forced it down, focusing instead on how gentle he'd always been with her. How patient. With Jason, she'd felt a level of pleasure she'd never realized she was capable of reaching. When he kissed her she felt hot and quivery from the inside out. Maybe it would be different this time, with this man. Maybe. She prayed that was true.

"You're worried about making love, aren't you?"

She nodded.

"I'd never hurt you, Charlotte. I hope you understand that. Whatever the problem is, we'll work it out together."

"I'm grateful…for that." Despite the excitement she felt at his kisses, she had to fight back the fear that threatened to choke her every time he mentioned the physical aspects of their relationship.

Her only recourse was to insist on a long engagement. That way she could slowly, gradually, feel comfortable with their sexual relationship. After they made love… She hesitated. There'd been a time she wouldn't have thought that was possible, but Jason had given her hope.

"Do you want to set the wedding date?" she asked, deciding to broach the subject now.

"Yes, but…" He shrugged. "There's one small problem."

"What's that?"

"I'm going to let my parents tell you. It's only fair. They're at home, waiting for us now."

Eleven

"I don't believe this!" Jason muttered under his breath as they pulled into his parents' driveway.

"What are all these cars doing here?" Carrie asked from the backseat. Jason had insisted on going back to the apartment to pick her up.

"You'll see," he said grimly.

Either his parents owned a car dealership or they were entertaining a houseful of company.

"This is going to be a real circus." He sighed as he helped Charlotte out of the front seat. Carrie bounded out from the back.

Charlotte's nervousness, already heightened by the prospect of an audience, grew exponentially.

The door opened and Elizabeth Manning

stepped out of the house. Jason's father and brothers, sisters-in-law and several children all crowded on the front porch behind her. The porch light revealed a variety of expressions, from amusement to elation.

"Well?" his mother asked as she walked toward them.

Jason slid his arm around Charlotte's waist and slowly, sweetly smiled down at her. In those brief seconds, Charlotte was comforted and reassured by his love. Her senses sang and her heart fluttered wildly.

Jason lowered his head. Charlotte wasn't sure that kissing in front of his parents, his whole family, was the best thing to do. Oh, what the heck. She was marrying Jason. They were in love, so a simple kiss shouldn't offend anyone.

Their lips met and she moaned a little with surprise and wonder at the ready response he never failed to evoke from her. Her hand crept up his chest and gripped the lapel of his suit jacket as his mouth made love to hers.

When he broke away, he was breathless. For that matter, so was Charlotte. She marveled that he was able to speak at all. "Does that answer your question, Mother?"

"Charlotte's agreed to marry you?"

"In a heartbeat," she answered for herself.

"Isn't it great!" Carrie shouted.

Spontaneous applause broke out from the porch, followed by several earsplitting whistles. Ryan and Ronnie were pounding their feet but she doubted the little boys understood exactly what the family was celebrating.

The evening was lovely; honeysuckle and roses scented the air. The sun had almost set, casting—literally—a rosy glow over the scene.

Jason bowed as though he were a knight and she his lady, accepting his family's enthusiasm.

"I hope you realize you're getting the runt of the litter," Paul told her, laughing.

"Hey," Rich put in. "Just be grateful that Charlotte's willing to put Jason out of his misery. He's been walking around like a lovesick puppy for weeks."

Jason glowered at his brothers, but she could tell he wasn't angry. He took their teasing in stride. From the time he'd brought her to that first softball game, Charlotte had envied him his family, especially the close relationship he shared with his brothers. The three were more than brothers; they were best friends. They looked out for one another and, just as important, they laughed together.

Leah and Jamie were best friends, too. Yet they seemed eager to extend that camaraderie to Charlotte. They'd gone out of their way to include her, to make her feel welcome, a part of the family. One of them.

Jason's mother came forward, tears in her eyes as she hugged Charlotte. "I couldn't be more pleased. Jason couldn't have chosen better."

"Thank you," Charlotte said, blushing. Doubt bobbed like a cork to the surface of her mind. Not that she didn't love Jason. She did, with all her heart, but she still wasn't sure whether she was the right woman for him.

"I'm so happy for you—and for us," Jamie said, hugging her next. "The two of you are perfect for each other. Leah and I agreed on that the minute we saw you together."

A warmth permeated Charlotte's heart. She wanted so badly to believe it was true.

"We'll be sisters now," Leah whispered, taking Charlotte's hands and lightly squeezing her fingers.

"I couldn't be marrying into a more wonderful family," Charlotte said to Jason as they made their way into the house. Carrie followed, carrying Jeremy, while the other children raced excitedly ahead.

His brothers congratulated Jason, slapping him on the back.

Once inside, Jason and Charlotte sat on the couch and the family gathered around them, making them the center of attention. Every eye was on Charlotte, smiling and happy, yet expectant. Puzzled, she glanced up at Jason, wondering if they wanted her to say something, to make some speech or pronouncement.

"Does she know yet?" Paul asked.

"No," Jason murmured. "I'm leaving the explanation up to Mom and Dad."

"Smart boy," Rich said, sitting on the armrest of the couch. He leaned forward eagerly, as though waiting for the opening act of an award-winning play.

"What's everyone talking about?" she asked.

"Mom?" Jason gestured eloquently toward his mother.

Elizabeth hesitated and turned to her husband. Eric Manning grinned and gave his wife a reassuring nod, which only compounded Charlotte's curiosity.

"As I said, I'm delighted that you've agreed

to marry Jason," Elizabeth began. "He's waited all this time to meet the right woman and, frankly, Eric and I were beginning to wonder if that was ever going to happen. Now that we've met you, Charlotte, we're glad he waited so long. We understood the moment we saw you together how special you were to him."

A low murmuring chorus of assent brought a sheen of tears to Charlotte's eyes. If anyone should be grateful, it was her. Jason had changed her world, opened her mind to everything she'd believed was closed off to her. Love. Family. Joy. Partnership.

The room went strangely quiet. Charlotte looked around and, although everyone seemed genuinely pleased, there was a tension here, too.

"Just tell her, Mother," Jason advised. "No need to drag this out."

By now, Charlotte was more than curious. "Tell me what?"

"Don't rush me," Elizabeth said, chiding her son. "Charlotte," she began, "when Jason told us he'd fallen in love with you, his father and I naturally wondered about his intentions. Then he told us he intended to ask you to marry him, so we decided to do a bit of checking in regard to the arrangements. Weddings need to be planned."

Jason's fingers entwined with hers, his hold on her hand tightening.

Elizabeth paused as though she expected a response. "Well, yes," Charlotte said, since everyone was staring at her. "That's a practical thing to do."

"I learned some distressing news," his mother continued. "The yacht club, which we feel is the best place for the reception, is booked solid for the next twenty-three months."

Once again, like clockwork, all eyes in the room swiveled to Charlotte, awaiting her response. "I hope you put our name on a waiting list, then," she murmured.

Elizabeth brightened, and some of the tension lines on her forehead seemed to relax. "I did better than that. You see," she went on, her voice growing more confident, "there happened to be a cancellation, and so I asked they reserve that day for you and Jason."

"Wonderful."

"You're leaving out the most important part," Jason said, his lips barely moving.

"The date is July fourteenth," Elizabeth announced, folding her hands and nodding sagely. "Don't you think that's excellent timing?"

"That sounds fine," Charlotte agreed, when it was apparent once again that everyone was waiting for her to respond. A little more than a year would give her and Jason ample time to discover if a marriage between them was viable. By then, they'd certainly know if a sexual relationship was possible. A year gave them both an opportunity to adjust.

"It's not July fourteenth of *next* year," Jason filled in, his gaze locking with hers. "Mother meant July fourteenth of *this* year."

Charlotte was too stunned to respond, other than with a gasp. Her mouth fell open in shock.

"What's the problem, Mom?" Carrie asked, looking surprised.

"But…but no one can plan a wedding of any size in that length of time," Charlotte managed after a moment. "It's…impossible."

"Not for Elizabeth," Leah said, her eyes sparkling with excitement. "Mom's been working on this since Jason mentioned the word *marriage*."

"But…"

"I've seen to everything," Elizabeth said confidently. "And it *is* possible, very possible—if you'll agree to such a quick wedding. I realize we're being unfair to you, and I do hope you'll find it in your heart to forgive me for taking over like this. The thing is, I know my son, and once he makes up his mind, that's the end of it. Jason wouldn't have been willing to wait almost two years."

"But…there are other places. Besides the yacht club, I mean."

"Yes, but none of them are as special."

"Charlotte," Jason said, raising her hand to his lips and kissing it. "I know it sounds crazy, but Mom's right. I wouldn't have wanted to wait just so my mother could put on a fancy wedding. At first I thought she'd gone berserk. The idea's preposterous, but the more I thought about it, the more I liked it."

"Leah and I will do anything we can to help," Jamie inserted. "If you want the truth, we're both thrilled."

"Taylor and Christy and their families are flying out. They've already made their reservations," Elizabeth added.

"But they can change them," Jason told her, frowning at his mother as if to say Charlotte was under enough pressure as it was.

And he was right. She felt as if a giant hammer was poised above her head, ready to smash down on her at any second. The entire family was waiting. Happy. Excited. Thrilled. Carrie's eyes begged her to say yes.

"Of course, Taylor and Christy can change their reservations, if necessary," someone said. That was Paul, and Charlotte wanted to thank him.

"Personally, I think it's wildly romantic," Leah added. She was sitting in the recliner, her hand resting on her swollen abdomen. Paul was sitting on the armrest, his arm wrapped around his wife's shoulders, his eyes filled with love as he gazed down on her.

"Naturally I haven't made any final decisions—that would be up to you," Elizabeth said.

"I...don't know what to say."

"You must think I'm a domineering old woman, and I suppose I am, but nothing's been finalized. I don't generally meddle in my children's lives, but—"

"Actually, if you want to be angry with anyone, it should be with the rest of us," Jamie told her. "Jason is the family's last chance for Mom to put on a big wedding. She'd been looking forward to it for years and we all disappointed her. She's always done a fabulous job with the receptions, though."

"We've had our hearts set on a formal wedding for so long," Eric said.

"But in three weeks?" Charlotte murmured.

"We'll all need to work together, of course, but we can do it." Jason's mother sounded utterly convinced of that. Her eyes sought out Charlotte's and, in their beautiful blue depths, Charlotte saw how much Elizabeth wanted this. How much the entire family did. They all looked forward to contributing.

"Charlotte," Jason said softly, "would you like more time to decide?"

She glanced around; everyone was waiting. The room had gone completely silent; even the children were quiet. Charlotte didn't know how she could refuse. She closed her eyes and tried to think. If she postponed the wedding, the elder Mannings might hold it against her. It could taint their future relationship. The others were just as eager for this to happen. Each one felt guilty for cheating Eric and Elizabeth out of the family wedding they wanted.

Her whole future with the Manning family could be at stake, Charlotte thought.

"Do I...need to decide now?" she asked after an awkward moment.

"There's so little time," Elizabeth warned.

Charlotte glanced from one to the other and knew she couldn't refuse. She loved Jason and wanted to marry him more than she'd wanted anything in her life. She could be happy with him, happy in ways she'd hardly imagined before. And for the first time she and Carrie had the chance to be part of a real family.

If she were to marry Jason there was the possibility of her having another child. *If* she conquered her fear of sex. The hollow ache inside her intensified as she studied the soft swell of Leah's abdomen.

She turned to Jason, needing some kind of confirmation, some indication of what he was thinking. His eyes, so like his mother's, blue and intense, reflected his love for her. His faith in her. The desire to be part of *her* life. He believed their love was enough to overcome any obstacle. Their love was all that was necessary.

For now, because she wanted to believe it, too, that was enough for her, too.

"We have a lot to do, then, don't we?" she said, reluctantly dragging her gaze away from Jason and back to his mother.

"Does that mean you agree?"

She nodded and the entire family broke into cheers.

The excitement and the enthusiasm carried Charlotte for a full two weeks. Two of the busiest weeks of her life. When she wasn't putting in her final days at work, she was with Jason's mother.

During their first afternoon together, it became apparent that Elizabeth was a gifted organizer. She'd have to be in order to pull off a full-scale wedding in less than a month.

Ignorance had been bliss. Had Charlotte realized the sheer magnitude of what they needed to accomplish in such a short time, she would have refused.

Not a day passed that she didn't have some kind of appointment, some place to be, someone to meet, some decision to make. There were dressmakers, florists, photographers, caterers and printers. And countless decisions, all of which had to be dealt with right that minute. There wasn't time to ponder or reflect. As soon as one task was completed, Elizabeth steered her toward the next.

Carrie was delighted to be her mother's maid of honor. Charlotte's four soon-to-be sisters-in-law were to be her bridesmaids, and that meant frequent conference calls between Montana and Seattle.

When Charlotte somehow found time to see Jason, it was for a few moments, and then only in passing. He, too, was exceptionally busy.

Just when it looked like everything was falling neatly into place, and Charlotte would finally be able to return to a life of her own, a series of showers and parties began. Every night was busy with one event or another. Even the women in the office held a bridal shower for her on her last day with the agency.

The Mannings were a well-established, well-liked family. Three of Elizabeth's closest friends decided to honor Charlotte with a shower the Monday before the wedding.

"I can't believe how generous everyone is," Charlotte said to Carrie, who had just attended the shower with her. They were carrying the wide array of gifts from the car into the apartment.

"Those old ladies don't even know you," Carrie remarked, her voice filled with astonishment. "All these gifts! You don't suppose they'd throw a birthday party for me sometime, do you?"

"Carrie!"

"Just joking, Mom." She hurried past Charlotte and brought in a gaily decorated box that was still unopened. Charlotte had been told the gift was for Jason, therefore he should be the one to open it. The giver was his godmother, a spry older woman named Donna Bondi.

"You want me to see if Jason's home?" Carrie asked eagerly.

Charlotte, too, was curious to see what was inside. "Go ahead." It was almost ten, and under normal circumstances Charlotte would've been more concerned about getting to bed so she'd be ready for work in the morning, but her two-weeks' notice was up and she was officially among the unemployed.

She had the entire week free, or as free as any bride's time could be five days before her wedding.

Carrie returned a few minutes later with Jason in tow. He smiled when he saw her and kissed her lightly on the lips, then bent to stroke an ecstatic Higgins. "What's this I hear about Mrs. Bondi sending me a gift?"

"She insisted you open it yourself."

Jason's look was skeptical. "Is it a gag gift?"

"I don't know. Why don't you find out?" Charlotte leaned against the kitchen counter and crossed her arms. "When you're finished, I'll show you all the loot we collected. I had no idea everyone would be so extravagant."

"Don't get any ideas about spending our honeymoon writing thank-you notes," he warned. He was grinning but she caught a serious undertone.

The honeymoon.

She wanted to talk to Jason about that, *needed* to talk to him about it, but there'd been so little time. They'd each been caught up in a whirlwind of activity. Since the evening he'd taken her to dinner and proposed, she hadn't spent any uninterrupted time with him. Now wasn't good, either. He was tired and so was she. Perhaps they could arrange to have lunch one day later this week.

Jason tore at the paper.

"You wouldn't believe Mom," Carrie said, her hands on the back of a kitchen chair as she looked on excitedly. "She doesn't tear a single piece of wrapping paper."

"It's all so pretty," Charlotte defended herself. "And I can use it again."

"It takes her forever to unwrap anything. I had to help her tonight, or we'd still be there."

Jason paused when he uncovered a plain white box. He raised his eyes to Charlotte.

"Don't look at me. I have no idea what Mrs. Bondi sent you."

Carefully he raised the lid and folded back the white tissue paper, but Charlotte couldn't see what was inside with Carrie bending over the table.

"All right, Mrs. Bondi," Jason said, emitting a low whistle.

Carrie covered her mouth and giggled before glancing at her mother.

"What is it?" Charlotte asked.

"Wait until you see this, Mom."

Using both hands, holding on to the thin straps, Jason lifted the sheerest, slinkiest, blackest nightie Charlotte had ever seen.

Charlotte forced a smile but she felt as though the older woman had slapped her in the face.

Charlotte knew better than to even try to sleep.

The next morning she'd walk down the church aisle and pledge her life to Jason Manning. She would vow to love and honor this man who'd come to mean so much to her.

To love him....

What would happen if she couldn't love him properly? What would happen when he realized she was incapable of satisfying him sexually? Would he claim he'd been cheated the way Tom had? Would he seek out another woman who'd give him the gratification she couldn't?

Oh, please, not that, not again—she couldn't bear it.

Charlotte didn't know how Jason would react, but she knew she'd find out soon.

She stared at the bright green numbers on her clock radio as one in the morning became two and then three.

The alarm was set for six. Charlotte's stomach tightened and a cold sweat broke out on her forehead. Her happiness had been supplanted by her fears, her anxieties and the certainty that her heart would be broken once again.

She'd made an effort to talk to Jason several times, she reasoned. It wasn't like she'd *planned* it this way. In the past week alone she'd called him three times, but he'd been so busy with his practice, tying up the loose ends so he'd have two uninterrupted weeks for their honeymoon in Hawaii.

The honeymoon terrified her even more than the wedding.

What was she supposed to do? Wait for Jason to say "I do," before she whispered in his ear that she wasn't sure she could satisfy him? Or should she say something before he slipped the ring on her finger?

It seemed cruel to wait until they got to their honeymoon suite. How could she possibly tell him something like that wearing the sheer black nightie Mrs. Bondi had sent?

The tightening in her stomach grew worse, until she thought she might actually throw up.

She shouldn't have left it to the last minute like this, but she'd had no other options.

She'd tried to spend time alone with Jason, to talk to him, but they hadn't connected all week. Whenever she saw him, there were other people around. She'd decided to demand time with him after the wedding rehearsal. They had to talk.

Only that hadn't worked, either.

They'd sat next to each other at the rehearsal dinner, but before she could say more than a few words, his brothers had spirited him away for a bachelor party.

Although she hadn't been in any mood to socialize, Charlotte had pretended to have a good time with Leah, Jamie, Jason's two sisters from Montana and her future mother-in-law. If any of them noticed how distracted she was, they must have attributed it to nerves.

By now the bachelor party would be over, probably had been for hours.

What was she going to do?

Her dinner, what little she'd eaten, soured in her stomach and she thought she might be sick. Tossing back the sheets, she climbed out of bed, waiting for the nausea to subside, then wandered aimlessly into the living room.

Dragging the afghan from the back of the sofa, she wrapped it around her shoulders and huddled in the recliner, the dog at her feet. Carrie and Mandy, Russ Palmer's half sister, were in the bedroom down the hall sleeping soundly, unaware of her torment.

Jason knew so little about her first marriage. He hadn't asked for information, and she'd volunteered even less. Instead, he'd cautiously tried to learn the details, but she'd put off explaining, afraid she'd lose him.

Soon, within less than twenty-four hours, Jason would know for himself why Tom had gone to another woman. Charlotte would have to face her inadequacies all over again.

As she sat in the dark, the shadows from the street danced against the walls, taunting her, jeering, shouting that she was a fool to believe she could ever satisfy a man.

Another hour passed and still the trapped, restless feeling refused to leave her; if anything, it became more intense. If only she could sleep. If only she could disappear. Vanish. Go someplace where no one would find her.

Squeezing her eyes shut, she tried to force her body to relax, but closing her eyes was just one more mistake. In her mind, Tom rose, scorn engraved on his handsome features. A cocky smile lifted the edges of his mouth, as if to tell her this was exactly what he'd been waiting for. As soon as she tried to make love with another man, she'd know everything he'd told her was true. *He* wasn't the one to blame for the failure of their marriage; she was. Charlotte—a woman too cold, too stiff, too lacking in sensuality.

Her eyes shot open and hot tears dripped down her face. A series of sobs racked her shoulders and took control of her body until she was trembling from head to foot.

She couldn't bear it, couldn't deal with it.

Tom was right, he'd always been right. She was a fool to believe that a sexual relationship between her and Jason would be any different, any better. They could kiss without a problem, but after the wedding, he was going to expect a lot more than a few kisses.

Panic filled her lungs, and it was all she could do not to scream in sheer terror.

Jason was wrapped in a warm cocoon of blankets, but the irritating noise refused to go away. He reached out his hand to turn off the alarm, fumbling with the dials before he realized it wasn't his alarm.

Opening one eye, he read the digital readout and discovered it was only four. He was entitled to another couple of hours' sleep. His head throbbed. Who'd come up with the bright idea of a morning wedding, anyway? No one had asked *him* about it.

The noise increased. It was now a steady pounding.

Someone was at his door. If this was one of his brothers' idea of a joke, he wasn't amused. He'd only gotten a few hours' sleep so far. If anyone in his family was involved in this, he'd make his displeasure clear in no uncertain terms.

Apparently whoever was at his door wasn't leaving. Jason struggled out of bed, pulled on a pair of pants and walked blindly through his apartment.

"Who is it?" he demanded irritably, wiping a hand down his face.

"Carrie."

"And Mandy."

The two vaulted into the room as he opened the door.

"You've got to do something!" Carrie cried.

Although his vision was a bit fuzzy, he could tell that she'd been crying.

"We didn't know what to do," Mandy wailed.

"About what?"

"This." Carrie handed him an envelope with his name written across the front. He recognized the handwriting as Charlotte's, but her usually smooth script was jerky and uneven.

Puzzled that she'd resort to writing a letter and having it delivered in the wee hours of the morning by two worried teenagers, he removed the single piece of paper.

He read it quickly.

Jason,
I'm sorry seems so inadequate, but I can't go through with the wedding. Please, if you can, find it in your heart to forgive me.

She'd signed it with her name.

It was a joke. Not a very good one, but he'd laugh over it in a few minutes.

"Who put you two up to this?" he asked, using his sternest voice.

"No one!" Carrie sobbed. "It's true. I got up to go to the bathroom and Mom's bedroom light was on, so I went in to see what was wrong and she wasn't there. She wasn't anywhere."

"The car's gone, too," Mandy added.

The words galvanized Jason into action. He shook the hair out of his face.

"What are we going to do?" Carrie asked, still crying softly.

"*We* aren't doing anything," Jason answered firmly.

"But someone has to do something!"

"I'll take care of it," he assured them. "Don't breathe a word of this to anyone, understand?"

"But…"

"Just do as I say. There isn't time to argue. If I'm not back with Charlotte before the car comes to take her to the church, tell everyone she's with me."

"What are you going to do?" Mandy asked, her eyes following him as he trotted back to his bedroom. He turned back and grinned. "Do?" he repeated. "Find her, of course. She's got a wedding to attend."

Twelve

Jason couldn't even guess where Charlotte was. He finished dressing, grabbed his car keys and took off, determined to find her.

He drove around for an hour, considering various possibilities. He tried to think like she would. If he were a bride running away from a wedding, where would he go? But that didn't work; he'd never run away from anything in his life, certainly not a wedding.

Darned if he knew what Charlotte was thinking. He had difficulty enough understanding women under normal circumstances. Still, he'd thought Charlotte was different. He'd thought—he'd assumed, erroneously it seemed—that Charlotte was as eager for their wedding as he was. He was shocked that he'd been so blind to her doubts. She must be terrified to have run away like this. Terrified and alone.

He should've known something like this would happen. He'd backed her into a corner, pushed her into this wedding. He'd allowed his own needs, his own desires, to overrule hers.

As dawn streaked the horizon with lavender and pink, he found himself growing ever more concerned.

Where could she be?

His driving became increasingly reckless, his speed gaining as he raced desperately from one possible location to the next. Checking the time, he was nearly swallowed by panic.

There wasn't much time left. They were both supposed to be at the church in a couple of hours. The thought of hurrying back to his family and having to announce that Charlotte had run away filled him with a sick kind of dread. He wouldn't return, he decided, until he'd found her. Until he'd done whatever he could to calm her fears, to reassure her, convince her how much he loved her.

Jason wasn't sure what led him to the beach where he'd proposed to her.

When he saw her car parked haphazardly

along the side of the road, he nearly collapsed in relief. A calmness took hold of him and his pulse slowed to an even, steady pace.

He parked behind her and rushed out of his car. The sound of the door closing must have been carried away with the wind, because she didn't turn around or give any indication that she realized he was there.

He paused for a few seconds, looking at her, his heart swelling with gratitude at finding her safe.

Charlotte sat on a log, facing the water. The same log he'd knelt in front of to ask her to marry him. He felt a stab of pain as he remembered that night and how ecstatic he'd been when she accepted his proposal. He didn't expect to feel that good again until they shared in the birth of a child.

Charlotte's shoulders were slumped forward and she seemed mesmerized by the gentle lapping of the water. The wind whipped her hair, which flew wildly about, but she didn't appear to notice. She wasn't wearing a sweater. She must be half freezing, Jason thought, peeling off his jacket.

He watched her for another moment, wondering exactly what he'd say. He'd had hours to prepare for this, hours to come up with the words to tell her how much he loved her and how sorry he was for the way everything had gone. Now he found himself speechless.

She didn't see him until he was almost upon her. When she happened to look up, he saw that her face, ravaged by tears, was as pale as moonlight. She blinked, then frowned as though she couldn't quite believe he was really there.

"Jason?"

"Funny meeting you here," he said, placing his jacket around her shoulders.

"I... How did you find me?"

"It took some effort. If you had any doubts, Charlotte, I wish you'd talked them over with me."

She frowned again. "There wasn't any time... I tried, honestly I did, but you were always so busy and the time went so fast, and now..." The rest of her words faded into nothingness, her gaze avoiding his.

"There's time now," he said, sitting down on the log beside her.

Her eyes widened. "I...can't go through with it."

"Why not?" he asked calmly.

She answered him with a wrenching sob. "Please...I can't. I don't love you..."

Jason tensed. "I don't believe that, Charlotte. There's something else."

"There is… I realize now that it's your family I love. I never had one of my own and it came to me that I was marrying you for all the wrong reasons. I…can't go through with the wedding… I just can't."

Jason felt as if someone had punched him. Hard. "My…family?"

"Yes," she cried. "They're all so wonderful and I…got carried away, thinking that if I married you…Carrie and I would be part of a large, loving family. Then I saw how unfair I was being to *you*…marrying you when I didn't love you."

A cold anger took hold of Jason. An anger rooted in pain and disillusionment.

"It's too bad you didn't think of that sooner, because all this soul-searching is a little too late." He grasped her arm and pulled her to her feet. She sagged against him, but he tugged at her and she straightened.

"Jason, please…"

"Shut up, Charlotte. Just shut up before I say something I'll regret." It was no comfort realizing she was the only woman who'd ever brought him willingly to his knees. He'd gone to her in love, a love so strong it had swept away his loneliness. Charlotte was throwing it all back at him now, rejecting his love, betraying him with her last-minute revelations.

Walking out on him at the eleventh hour like this couldn't be considered anything less. Nothing she could've done would have humiliated him more than to leave him standing at the altar.

"I can't be your wife... Don't you understand?"

Her voice was so weak he wasn't sure he'd heard her correctly. Not that it mattered; nothing she could have said would've had any effect on him after her confession. It didn't matter if he could hear her or not. She was mumbling, pleading with him, but he closed off his heart the same way he had his ears.

When they reached his car, he opened the passenger door and deposited her inside. He ran around to the driver's side, not knowing if he could trust her to stay put. He was mildly surprised that she didn't try to escape.

He started the engine and turned on the heater. A blast of warm air filled the car. She didn't seem to notice.

Neither spoke until they were close to the freeway entrance.

"Why are you doing this?" she demanded.

"I don't know," he answered. "But I do know you're going through with this wedding, if it's the last thing either of us ever does."

"But how can you force me to marry you, knowing what you do?"

"It must have something to do with saving my entire family from humiliation," he continued with the same chilly irony. "That family you claim to love so much. Maybe it's because I don't want my mother—who's worked day and night on this wedding for the past three weeks, who's looked forward to this day for years—to become an object of pity among her friends. Maybe it's because I'd have trouble looking my two sisters and their husbands in the eye, knowing they rearranged their entire summer, gave up their vacations, to fly out here for our wedding. Just maybe it's because I have an aversion to being ridiculed myself. I can't really tell you what else would reduce a man to drag a woman who's rejected him to the altar. But make no mistake, Charlotte, you will marry me."

"It isn't that I don't care for you," she whispered through her tears.

"Right. You care so deeply that you decided to go into hiding on our wedding day."

"I know you're angry…"

"You're damn right I'm angry."

"We can't go through with the wedding, Jason! We just can't."

"Oh, but we are, Charlotte."

"What will we do afterward? I mean, once we're married and—"

"Somehow we'll find a way to miss our flight to Hawaii, then, first thing Monday morning, I'll file for an annulment."

"But it doesn't make sense to go through with the wedding—"

"Yes, my darling Charlotte, it does. It makes a whole lot of sense."

Charlotte was determined to survive the day, although she wasn't sure how she'd manage. She'd been a fool to run off the way she had. A fool and a coward. She was an even bigger fool to think she'd appease Jason's anger by lying.

When she'd left, she hadn't thought about what she was doing to Jason or his family. She hadn't been thinking at all, overpowered instead by her own fears.

On the way back, she tried to tell Jason she was sorry, to apologize for the hurt and humiliation she'd caused, but each time he cut her off, saying he didn't want to hear it.

The ride back to her apartment was like living through the worst nightmare of her life. Jason was so cold, so furiously angry.

He dropped her off at her apartment, took her arm, leveled his steely blue eyes on her and said, "I'll be by to pick you up in forty minutes."

"I can't possibly be ready by then."

"You can and you will. And, Charlotte, don't even think about running away again. Do you understand me?"

Charlotte nodded and almost told him it was bad luck for the groom to see the bride before the wedding. Then she remembered the whole wedding was a farce, anyway.

"Fine. I'll be ready," she assured him calmly.

She showered, brushed her hair and dressed, but she wasn't conscious of doing any of those things. Carrie was with her, and Mandy, too, both silent and pale. Worried. What she'd done to them was terrible, Charlotte realized. They were both too young to carry this secret, too young to bear the burden of her foolishness.

Neither girl asked her any questions, and

for that, Charlotte was grateful. She didn't know what she would've told them if they had.

Leah and Jamie had arrived within minutes of Jason's bringing her home. They were both happy and excited. If her complete lack of emotion bewildered them, they didn't let it show. They chatted excitedly, recalling events at their own weddings, bubbling over with enthusiasm. Charlotte tried to smile, tried to pretend this was the happiest moment of her life. Leah and Jamie seemed to believe it, even if the girls had their doubts.

Jason arrived to escort her to the church, and her future sisters-in-law shooed him away. She wore the beautiful off-white dress Elizabeth Manning had insisted on buying her, and Leah had woven flowers in her hair.

Before she knew it, Charlotte was at the church. The number of guests surprised her. Tears clogged her throat when she reminded herself that she was playing a role. Tomorrow morning she'd go back to what her life had been before she met Jason Manning. Back to the emptiness. The loneliness.

At the appropriate moment, with organ music swirling around her, she walked dutifully down the aisle, aware every second of Jason standing at the front of the church. His eyes held hers as effectively as a vise, as though he suspected she might try to run even now. And if she tried, she didn't doubt for a second that he'd go after her.

With her morning little more than a vague memory, Charlotte found it ironic that the actual wedding ceremony was so clear to her.

Jason stood at her side, revealing no emotion, and calmly repeated his vows. Charlotte wondered why the minister didn't stop him. It was all too evident from the clipped, angry tone of his voice that he didn't mean what he was saying. He had no intention of loving her, of cherishing her, of allowing her ever to be important in his life. Not after what she'd done. Not after she'd led him to believe her motives were so deceitful. Not after she'd made him think she planned to ridicule him and his family. Whatever love he'd once felt for her was dead. He'd practically told her so himself.

When it was her turn to say her vows, Charlotte's voice was surprisingly strong. She would always love Jason, and she'd always treasure the months they'd shared. The sincerity in her voice must have caught his attention, because he looked at her for the first time since they'd approached the altar. His eyes narrowed scornfully. For a moment she nearly faltered, but decided she wouldn't let him intimidate her.

His eyes seemed to be laughing at her—a mocking laugh that told her she was the biggest hypocrite who'd ever lived. He could think what he wanted, but in her heart she knew the truth.

After the ceremony, they were whisked from the church to the reception at the yacht club.

For Charlotte, the lengthy reception was a thousand times worse than the ceremony. They stood, for what seemed like hours, with the members of their wedding party, while an endless line of guests paraded past.

Everyone was so thrilled for them, so happy, everyone except the two of them. From the moment they'd arrived at the reception, Charlotte was a heartbeat away from dissolving into tears. Heaven knew how she survived the ordeal.

Later they had to cut the cake. The photographer took picture after picture.

"Resist the urge to shove the cake in my face," Jason whispered behind a smile, when she went to feed him a small piece for the camera, "and I'll do the same."

They ate, they danced, they opened gifts. Outwardly they were the perfect couple. Madly in love, solicitous of each other, eager to be alone. Eager to start their lives together.

Only Charlotte and Jason knew the reality beneath the pretense.

Despite herself, Charlotte was impressed by what a brilliant actor Jason was. He refrained from touching her, but when it was unavoidable, his arms were gentle, his look as tender as he could make it, although she knew that he seethed with outrage. She could feel his anger, hidden below the surface, out of everyone's sight but hers. At times Charlotte felt as if that anger would devour her whole.

"Just a few minutes longer," Jason whispered harshly while they were on the dance floor. "Then we can leave."

She relaxed. "Where are we going?"

"Not the airport, so don't worry about it."

"We need to talk."

"No, we don't. Everything's been said. I'll drop you off at your apartment and you can forget this day ever happened."

"But—"

"Like I said, don't worry about it. I'll arrange everything. Once this is over, we won't ever have to see each other again. Needless to say, I'll expect you to find a new place as soon as possible."

She nodded, knowing she'd brought this on herself. But when it was time to go, there was a surprise awaiting both of them. Jason's brothers and brothers-in-law had rented two limousines. The first to take them to the airport, Rich explained, grinning proudly. And the second limousine was so the entire wedding party could follow them and see them off with as much fanfare and enthusiasm as was allowed.

Jason's eyes sought out Charlotte's when she returned from changing her clothes. His gaze assured her not to worry. He wasn't any more willing to spend two weeks in her company than she'd been about going through with the wedding. She was sure he'd find some way to miss the flight.

Except that he didn't.

His mother waited with them at the airline counter, wiping the tears from her eyes as she hugged her son. Carrie was there, too, more relaxed now, excited that she and Higgins would be spending two weeks with Leah and Paul.

Charlotte hugged Jason's mother farewell, tears brimming in her eyes. "No woman ever had a more beautiful wedding," she whispered. "Thank you."

Her father-in-law was waiting when she'd finished, holding out his arms to her as though she were a small child needing reassurance. Nothing could be closer to the truth.

"Eric, thank you," she murmured, as she slipped into his embrace. This might well be the only opportunity she'd have to express her gratitude. Soon enough Jason's parents would know. She wouldn't be able to face them.

"You call me Dad," Eric said, hugging her close. "We already love you like a daughter, Charlotte."

Tears blurred her vision and when she turned, she nearly collided with Jason. He took her by the elbow, his fingers pinching her skin. "You're laying it on a bit thick, aren't you?"

She didn't answer him, couldn't have said a word if she'd tried. They got their boarding passes as everyone watched. They were going to Hawaii, like it or not.

Charlotte realized there was no escape for them, unless they owned up to the truth immediately. Jason didn't look any more pleased than she did, but obviously didn't want to dis-illusion the family quite so soon.

As he led her into the security area, away from his family, he muttered, "I didn't plan this."

"I know," she said with a helpless sigh. "Oh—my car. I left it at the beach."

"Mandy's getting it for you."

His thoughtfulness surprised her. "Thank you."

"Don't mention it," he said sarcastically. "I wanted it back in the apartment lot so you wouldn't have any trouble leaving again. Next time you can go with my blessing."

Their seats were in business class and they were quickly served glasses of champagne that neither of them drank.

As the plane taxied away from the jetway and toward the airstrip, he closed his eyes, heaved a massive sigh and said, "Don't worry, I'll get us out of this yet."

Charlotte nodded and lowered her gaze. "I'll do everything I can to stay out of your way."

"That would be appreciated."

The flight was five hours, but it seemed closer to fifty. Jason didn't exchange one un-necessary word with Charlotte. At this rate, she didn't know how they'd be able to spend two weeks in each other's company.

Jason must have been thinking the same thing. "I'll see what I can do about arranging a flight back to Seattle as soon as we land," he told her briskly, without a shred of emotion. No regret, no disappointment, nothing.

Charlotte bit her lip. "I...I didn't pack much of anything...since the suitcase was just for show."

He didn't respond. By the time they landed and collected their luggage, Charlotte was falling asleep on her feet. Apparently Jason suspected as much, since he made some excuse about contacting the airlines from the hotel instead of rushing her onto a return flight. But she wasn't sure if this small kindness was for her benefit or his own, since he couldn't have had much more sleep than she had.

She barely noticed the scenery as the taxi carried them through town. Their hotel was on Waikiki Beach, built on white sands and surrounded by swaying palms.

When they went to check in at the front desk, Charlotte stepped back, letting Jason take care of the necessary paperwork. He was obviously upset about something, but she couldn't tell what.

"Is everything all right?" she asked, as they moved toward the elevator.

"I thought we could get a double room, but..." Jason rubbed a hand across his face, looking weary and defeated. "My parents booked us into the bridal suite."

"Oh." Charlotte didn't fully realize the implications of that until the bellman ushered them, with much fanfare, into the corner suite. There was one bed. A king-size bed that loomed before her.

Charlotte's startled gaze sought out Jason's as he paid the attendant and closed the door. The fear she'd managed to bury for hours spilled over now, but before she could say a word, he turned to her.

"Don't look so shocked. It isn't as if I intend to make love to you."

"But where will...we sleep?"

He laughed, the sound abrupt. "If you want to call down to the front desk and order a rollaway for the bridal suite, then by all means, be my guest. Frankly, I feel enough of a fool for one day, so I'll leave that option to you."

With no real alternative, she showered, put on an old T-shirt and crawled between the crisp sheets of the bed, making sure she was as far on her side as possible.

She was drifting off to sleep when Jason finished his shower and returned to the bedroom. He stood for several minutes looking down at her. Her heart roared like a crazed animal as she wondered about his intentions. He could force her. Tom had often enough, using her body, leaving her feeling sick and abused afterward. She'd curl up tightly while he shouted how incompetent she was, how unattractive, how lacking. She'd lie there silently as the ugly, demeaning words rained down on her. When he was done with his tirade he'd leave.

The memories made her shiver with revulsion and fear.

"Charlotte."

She didn't answer, pretending to be asleep. Jason was angry with her, angrier than she'd ever seen him. Eyes closed, she lay still, her heart pounding with dread.

She heard Jason dressing, heard him pause and then, after a moment, heard him turn off the light and leave the room.

Abruptly Charlotte sat up. He'd left her, walked away just like Tom had, as though he couldn't bear to be in the same room with her. Like Tom, he couldn't wait to be rid of her.

He'd left without a word.

Wasn't that what she wanted? Then why did she feel so alone, so deserted and unloved, so empty inside?

The tears that had threatened most of the day broke free with a low, eerie wail. She tucked her knees against her chest as the sobs overtook her.

She wept for all she'd lost. Jason's love. Any chance of sharing their lives. The dream of having another child. The family she'd never had. It was gone now, crushed by her own hand.

It was too late to try and get any of it back. Jason hated her. She could never recapture what she'd destroyed with her fear. Never rebuild the trust she'd demolished when she'd run away.

She sobbed until the well of grief was emptied. Even that wasn't enough. She tore at the sheets, pulling the blankets from the bed and beating the pillows.

It didn't take long to exhaust what little energy she had, and she fell across the bed sobbing, then fell into a deep, troubled sleep.

* * *

Jason came back to the room an hour later, moving as silently as possible, not wanting to wake Charlotte. He wished he could hate his wife, punish her for what she'd done. She deserved to suffer, didn't she?

But if that was really the case, then why was *he* the one in pain? He saw her climb into bed and curl up, and it was all he could do not to dash across the room and take her in his arms. This woman had betrayed him, and yet he wanted to comfort her.

It was either leave the room or beg her forgiveness for forcing her to endure this day. She wasn't entitled to his forgiveness, he reminded himself, which meant there was only one option. He'd left.

He'd gone for a walk on the beach, which wasn't exactly how he'd expected to spend his wedding night. Not that he was any great shakes as a husband. A hundred times or more he'd gone over his own part in this fiasco. He'd rushed Charlotte into marriage and so had his family, not giving her a chance for second thoughts. Looking back, he understood now that it was the urgency of his mother's idea that he'd found so appealing. Now he understood why.

He'd rushed into marriage with Charlotte because, deep down, he'd been afraid that if she'd had the chance to change her mind, she would. And he'd been right.

Jason didn't know what lunacy had prompted him to make her go through with the ceremony. To avoid embarrassment? Having their marriage annulled the following week would still embarrass him and his family. There was the problem, too, of returning all the wedding gifts. Eventually he'd have to face people. Make explanations.

He'd taken the easy way out, delaying the inevitable because of his pride.

Charlotte had wanted to cancel the wedding and he'd perversely refused to release her. So now they were stuck in Hawaii on a two-week honeymoon neither of them wanted. Stuck in each other's company, in the bridal suite no less, until he could find a flight back to Seattle.

Once his eyes had adjusted to the dark, Jason made his way across the elegant room. Charlotte was still curled up on the bed, but the sheets and blankets were strewn about as though a storm had raged through.

He discovered a second and a third pillow hurled across the room. One was on the floor, the other dangling from a chair. It looked as if his bride had thrown a temper tantrum.

So she hadn't liked it that he'd left. A smile played across his lips. It was the first time since he'd found her on the beach that she'd displayed any emotion.

The thought of Charlotte losing her temper pleased him, until he remembered she wasn't given to bouts of anger. He felt a pang of concern but brushed it aside—it belonged to the past, to the old Charlotte, the one he'd loved.

Exhausted and depressed, he gazed about the room and noted that the bed was all she'd bothered to disarrange. Everything else in the room remained untouched.

Not knowing what to think, and too tired to care, he quietly stripped off his clothes and slipped beneath a rumpled sheet. It didn't take him long to fall asleep, but his dreams were disturbing and he woke several times before morning.

Not once during the night did Charlotte move. She stayed on her side, facing away from him, never changing her position.

He woke in the morning, the bright sunshine slashing through the bedroom curtains. Charlotte was on her back, already awake. She shifted her head and stared at him with eyes so filled with pain that he hurt just looking at her.

"I lied when I said I didn't love you, Jason," she whispered and a tear rolled down the side of her face. "I do…so very much. I'm sorry… for everything I've done."

He nodded, his throat thick. "I'm sorry, too, Charlotte."

Thirteen

Charlotte closed her eyes because looking at Jason was so painful, knowing he hated her, knowing he'd never really forgive her for what she'd done.

"I lied when I said I wanted to marry you because of your family. I…ran away because I was afraid."

"Of me?"

Her pulse scampered. She should've told him the truth weeks earlier. She'd agreed to be his wife; he had a right to know. But the truth was so easy to put off, so easy to deny. So hard to explain.

There'd been opportunities to tell him, plenty of them, although she'd tried to convince herself otherwise. She'd been too much of a coward to present Jason with the truth. And then, when time ran out, she'd panicked.

"Charlotte?" Jason said in a low voice. "What are you afraid of?"

She couldn't explain that she was, to put it bluntly, afraid of sex. Of intimacy. That wasn't what a man wanted to hear. Not just Jason, but any man.

He deserved so much more than she was capable of giving him. He deserved a woman who was emotionally whole and healthy. A woman who was physically responsive. Not someone scared and battle-weary and all but dead to her own sexuality.

"I owe you an explanation...."

"I'd say so," he agreed, but his voice was devoid of the previous day's sarcasm, without a trace of anger.

"I meant to tell you sooner. To give you the choice of going through with the wedding or not. But as time went on I—I couldn't...and then it was too late."

"Tell me now."

Charlotte thought back to an age when she'd been innocent, vulnerable and naive. "My mother died while I was in high school. My father had abandoned us years earlier

Debbie Macomber

and I don't think my mother ever recovered. If he contacted her at any point after he left, I didn't know about it. She was different after he was gone. It was like she'd given up on life. She loved me, though—I know she did—and she'd been insightful enough to plan for my future."

Jason's hand reached across the bed for hers. Their fingers entwined and Charlotte was grateful for his touch.

"I met Tom my first year of college. He came from another state and was attending classes on a limited scholarship. He was intelligent and good-looking. When he asked me out, I was thrilled. He seemed to like me.... Later I realized it wasn't me that attracted him, but the insurance money I'd received when my mother died. After a few months, we made love and...and he asked me to marry him. I didn't have any family and...I desperately needed someone. I was too stupid to know why Tom really wanted to marry me. He saw marriage as a way of paying for his education without having to work for it.

"I dropped out of school after one semester and we got married. The money that was meant for my education went toward Tom's while I got a full-time job to pay our living expenses."

Jason's hand flinched, tightening around hers.

"I should've gotten out of the marriage as soon as I figured out he was using me. Instead, I compounded my mistake. I thought if I got pregnant it would make everything better. If Tom didn't love me, surely he'd love the baby."

"You've been so hard on yourself."

"I'll never regret having Carrie. She's been the best thing in my life...but Tom wasn't happy." She hesitated, reliving the terrible scene, so many years past, when she'd told Tom she was pregnant. He'd wanted her to have an abortion, even given her the money. She'd lied and told him she'd done it, hiding her pregnancy until it was too late. He'd been so furious that he'd hit her. The blow had been so hard, it had loosened three of her teeth.

"Go on," Jason prompted.

"I had Carrie and for a while I thought the marriage might work. Tom liked his little girl and was proud of her."

"You told me Tom was having an affair. When did this happen?"

"It started while I was pregnant. Tom enjoyed sex…and after a while he said I was too fat and ugly to make love to, and everything came to a stop." Charlotte remembered how relieved she was, how grateful because she no longer had to give in to his rough physical demands. She was working a forty-hour week, waiting tables, and was too exhausted at night to satisfy him. He'd been telling her for months that a man needed enthusiasm from his wife during sex, but Charlotte had never seemed able to rouse any. It was like making love to a corpse, he told her.

"I…I never was very good at sex," she continued in a tight voice. "And after Carrie was born, I lost all interest." Actually any pleasure in the physical aspects of their marriage had died months earlier, when Tom had demanded she have an abortion. After Carrie was born, she found herself unwilling to make any effort to please him physically.

"That was when the really bad fights began," she said as evenly as the remembered emotions would allow. "Tom claimed it was his right to make love to me whenever he wanted and…and…" Her throat closed up, forcing her to stop.

"Did he rape you, Charlotte?"

Biting her lower lip, she nodded. Only Tom hadn't called it rape; he'd said it was his right. He'd married her, hadn't he? That meant she'd given him the right to do whatever he wanted with her body the moment she'd signed the marriage document.

Jason moved closer and brought her into his arms, cradling her head against his shoulder, stroking her hair. His chest was heaving and Charlotte knew he was fighting his own anger.

Her eyes glazed over with tears as she struggled to hold back the fear, the memory of the violence, the feeling of powerlessness, the revulsion of those terror-filled episodes. Her breathing became labored.

"I...couldn't satisfy Tom," she admitted in a breathless whisper.

"That has everything to do with Tom—not with you." He paused. "Are you afraid you won't be able to satisfy me?"

She nodded through her tears.

"But, Charlotte," he said, raising himself on one elbow and gazing down at her, "how can you think that? Everything between us has always been so good. Or am I wrong? Haven't you enjoyed the times we kissed?"

She lowered her lashes. "Yes…but they've frightened me."

"I never forced you."

"I…I know that. You've been so patient and gentle. I almost convinced myself I could make love again…that I could erase those nightmare years with Tom and start all over… but I can't. That's why I ran away…that's the real reason, not what I told you earlier."

"Why couldn't you tell me this before?"

She wiped the tears from her face, and swallowed the bittersweet agony of the moment. "Because I love you so much."

Her words were met with a puzzled hesitation. "You wouldn't tell me because you love me?"

She nodded, and hiccuped a sobbing laugh. "It sounds ludicrous, I know, but it's true. Because I couldn't stand to lose you—not that way. Because if we ever did make love, you'd see—you wouldn't want me anymore."

"How could you think that?" Jason asked.

This was the moment she'd dreaded. The moment of truth. She turned her head away, unwilling to look at him, unwilling to let him see her face. A tightness gripped her chest, crushing her, the pressure so intense she could hardly breathe.

"Charlotte?"

It would've been easier if he hadn't been so gentle. She could deal with his anger and frustration, but not his tenderness. She didn't know how to respond to that in a man.

Shoving aside the blanket and sheet, she sat on the edge of the bed. When he caressed her back, she stood, unable to deal with being touched just then. Her arms were locked around her middle and the aching pressure in her chest rose, settling in her throat. Tears burned her eyes.

"Tell me," he demanded, not unkindly. "Just say it."

"I can't be your wife."

"It's too late for that," he murmured. "You already are."

"I'm not...not in the ways that matter to a man."

"Oh?"

"Don't you understand what I'm saying?" she cried. "Do I have to spell out every degrading detail? Is that what you want? Then fine, I'll say it. I can't be your wife because I can't make love." She gulped in a deep breath. "I'm frigid, Jason. The term might be out of fashion but it still applies."

There was a brief, shocked silence. Then Jason started to laugh.

"Don't you dare laugh at me! Don't you dare laugh." A fury rose inside Charlotte, one that had been years in the making, one so strong there was no holding back. She threw herself at him, arms swinging, feet kicking, fingers clawing, before he had a chance to react.

He caught her by the wrists. "Charlotte…I wasn't laughing at *you*."

She barely heard his words, not that it mattered. She twisted and bucked in his hold. He twisted, too, and with the momentum of his weight they fell together on the bed. He was sprawled over her upper body, his thigh across her legs, holding her down.

Her chest was heaving, her shoulders jerking upward in an effort to escape.

"Charlotte, for heaven's sake, I wasn't laughing at you," he said again.

She gritted her teeth, refusing to answer him.

"Stop struggling, before you destroy any chance of my fathering our future child."

She went still, although the fight hadn't completely left her.

"Now let me explain."

There were too many years of agony inside her, too many insecurities to be soothed away with a few simple words. "No. Just let me go."

"In a minute. Then if you still want me to release you I will. You owe me this much. All right?"

She twisted her head away from him, still refusing to answer.

"I love you, Charlotte. I realized when we first started seeing each other that you'd been badly hurt by your ex-husband. I didn't understand the extent of it until now, but in some ways I think not knowing was for the best. It would have intimidated me in the beginning."

A sob tore through her throat.

"The first time we kissed…I wish I knew how to explain it, but I knew you were different. That moment was different than any I'd ever known before. Kissing you was so good."

Charlotte didn't respond, but she knew he was right. Their kisses *had* been good. Very good.

"It got even better, didn't it?"

She nodded, although only slightly.

"You're not frigid, or whatever term the psychologists prefer now. Not even close.

What you are, my love, is afraid, and for a very legitimate reason. You've been sexually abused."

"I'm sexually...damaged. Forever."

"No, not forever. In time you'll heal. We'll heal together." He said it with such conviction, as though they faced only a small problem, when to her it was bigger than both of them. Bigger than even their love.

"But it isn't *you* who...can't make love," she sobbed. "It's me. You're not the one who has to heal...and I don't know if I can."

"We're in this together, Charlotte. Whatever it takes."

"There isn't any reason you should—"

"We can't heal," he interrupted, "unless we try. We can't sweep this under the carpet and ignore it. I'm not so stupid as to believe that all the pain and all the memories will go away simply because we make love and it's as good as our kisses have been."

"I...don't know if I'll ever be able to forget."

Jason rolled away from her, freeing her arms and legs. He stood and raked his hand through his hair. "The decision is yours, and I'll abide by whatever you want. I'm not going to force you to be my wife. I've made some mistakes in this relationship and just now was one of them. I'm sure I'll make more. You should know that."

"I don't understand what you're saying." She sat up and wiped the tears from her burning cheeks, her hands trembling. Jason had moved away from her and was staring out the window.

"Like I said, the decision is yours. If you want me to file for an annulment, then I will. I'll make the arrangements to get us off this island as quickly as possible. As soon as I can, I'll take care of all the legalities. In a few days there won't be anything to bind us together—if that's what you want."

"I see." Her heart filled with mourning.

"But there's something you should understand, Charlotte. If you decide you want to give this marriage a try, there'll be no turning back."

She did understand, and the thought filled her with panic.

"I'm willing to devote myself to you and the marriage, but I'll need the same kind of commitment from you. In other words, you're going to have to *want* to heal. It may mean counseling for you, for us both. We both have to be willing to do whatever it takes."

"I don't know if I could...ever tell anyone else about my marriage to Tom."

"That's your decision, too. If you want to stay my wife, you have to realize that the time will come when we *will* make love—but only when you're ready. And when we do, it'll be good, Charlotte...I promise you that."

"How often?" It was probably a stupid question, but one she needed to know. She might be able to bear it if Jason wanted to make love occasionally. She might be able to overcome the terror if he wasn't too demanding.

"I can't answer that because I don't know."

"More than once a month?"

He turned away from her, but not before she saw his smile. "Yes, Charlotte, more than once a month."

"I see."

"It seems to me that you have some serious thinking to do. Perhaps it would be best if I left for a while. When I come back, you can tell me your thoughts. Does that sound fair?"

She waited until he turned to look at her before she nodded.

So this was what it meant to love someone, Jason thought as he left the hotel and headed for the beach. He felt as though a hole had been carved through the center of his life, and nothing—besides Charlotte—was capable of filling it. He wanted to believe she'd realize he wasn't another Tom. That didn't seem to be the case, however.

He'd felt a glimmer of hope when he'd first started talking, trying to get through to her, soothe her fears. The anger had drained from her eyes as she'd studied him, seeming to measure his words. He'd seen trust gradually replace that anger.

He hoped she'd be willing to give their marriage a chance. He loved her, but he wasn't naive or arrogant enough to believe his feelings for her could, on their own, heal the horror of her experience. She was going to need more than his love, more than his gentleness. Being tender and patient with her wasn't going to wipe out the trauma of having been raped by her own husband. No wonder she was so terrified.

Jason sensed that other things, maybe even worse than those he knew, had happened in her marriage. Things she hadn't told him yet.

Her marriage had been so ugly, so abusive. He marveled that she'd even considered remarrying. Knowing what he did now, it didn't surprise him that she'd run away at the eleventh hour. It wouldn't surprise him if she decided to go through with the annulment, either.

He'd given her the option, laid everything out on the table for her to examine. His love, his commitment, his willingness to do whatever he could to help her overcome her fears. But in light of what he'd learned, it seemed so little....

A couple of hours later, Jason returned to the hotel to confront Charlotte again. Two hours didn't seem like much time to come to such a monumental decision, but he wanted to be with her.

Perhaps it would be best if he waited for her to come to him, but he quickly rejected that idea as impractical. If he was going to waste precious time debating with himself, he should do it over something important, like how was he going to live without Charlotte. How was he going to let her go, the only woman he'd ever truly loved? Those were the questions he should be asking himself.

Charlotte sat in the darkened room, the drapes pulled against the brightness of the sun, waiting for Jason. Having carefully considered her husband's words, she knew with a clarity that defied explanation what she was meant to do. She *should* remain his wife. *Should* share his bed. *Should* share his life.

The heavy ache in her chest intensified. Fresh tears moistened her eyes. Jason had offered her his love, his devotion, and his wholehearted commitment. He'd done so with a courage that left her humbled. He was willing to help her heal, but Charlotte didn't know if it would be enough.

There was no guarantee the pain would ever end. No guarantee she'd ever feel whole again. Healing demanded courage. It meant reaching back into the past, into the pain, and reliving the nightmare. Wasn't enduring it *once* enough? Healing meant risking whatever serenity she'd found in the years since her divorce. Healing meant trusting a man again, trusting him enough to freely share her body.

Charlotte closed her eyes, wanting to blot everything out. She was such a coward. A world-class wimp. She knew what she *should* do, but it was so frightening. She wanted to run away, bury her feelings. Hide, the way she'd been doing for years. There was something so comfortable in denial.

There had to be more to life than this choking anger. More than this grief and fear.

With Jason's love there *was* more.

There was hope.

Charlotte must have fallen asleep. When she stirred she saw that the drapes were open and Jason was sitting on the lanai, sipping a glass of orange juice.

"Hello," he said with a smile.

"Hi." She felt a little shy as she slipped out of bed and rubbed her eyes. "What time is it?"

"Afternoon. I imagine you're starved."

Now that he mentioned it, she realized she was hungry. The last food she'd eaten had been at their wedding dinner, and that had been the day before.

"I took the liberty of ordering you lunch."

She smiled and joined him on the lanai. "I slept for so long."

"You needed the rest." He looked so familiar and handsome, sitting there in the sunlight with his baseball cap shading his eyes. His skin was bronzed, and his eyes, as blue as the Hawaiian sky, roamed over her with undisguised love and tenderness. "Listen, Charlotte, I was wrong."

"Wrong?"

"I shouldn't have given you an ultimatum. You're going to need more than a few hours to decide what you want. I made the same mistake earlier by rushing you into a marriage you didn't want and..."

"But I did want this marriage, very badly."

"Did," he repeated in a husky, regretful voice.

"Do," she corrected firmly.

For several minutes, he said nothing. "Even now, knowing what it'll mean?"

"Even now," she said, holding out her hand to him.

Jason held it fast. "I love you, Charlotte Manning."

"I know." Her voice broke, and she struggled not to break down and weep. Someday she'd tell him how close she'd come to walking away from the brightest promise of her life. She'd tell him how she'd finally decided that loving Jason, being his wife, sharing his life wasn't just something she *should* do, but something she *wanted* to do. *Ached* to do, with all her heart. Someday she'd tell him all of this.

"I don't want to live without you."

He reached for her, bringing her onto his lap, his mouth instinctively finding hers. Everything she'd planned to say was caught between two hungry mouths. Trapped between two pounding hearts.

Fourteen

Several months later a storm, a Seattle cloud-burst, woke Charlotte. Dawn was on the horizon, but very little light filtered through the gray clouds. The wind beat hard against the windows, rattling them until Charlotte feared they might break.

Gently setting aside the covers, she climbed out of bed and crept into the living room. Higgins was sleeping there, looking worried. She patted his head and offered him reassurances.

She opened the living-room drapes just in time to watch a bolt of lightning rip apart the night. For an hour or so afterward, smiling contentedly, she watched morning creep across the sky. Her life, inside and out, was everything she wanted it to be. Jason had moved into her apartment; they planned to buy a house in the spring. She was taking a break from work, enrolled in an advanced accounting course. Eventually she'd handle all of his bookkeeping and maybe look for a few other clients, too. Yes, life was full of new possibilities.

"Charlotte?" Jason murmured when she returned to bed. He reached for her and without a second's hesitation she slipped into his embrace.

"There's a storm," she whispered.

His smile was lazy, sleepy. "So I hear. Are you frightened?"

"Not anymore." There'd been a time when she would've been terrified, but that time was long past. She felt intensely alive, completely calm. The dangerous storms were gone from her life. She'd survived the raging wind, the drenching rain, the booming thunder. That was all in the past. Her future was holding her in his arms.

She sighed, cuddling close to her husband, suffused with a feeling of profound joy.

"I love you," she whispered.

"I know," he said without opening his eyes. "Believe me, I know."

She slid her arms up his shoulders and brought her mouth to his. He welcomed her kiss, which was slow and deep. Hot excitement poured into her blood. Soon the kiss was no longer slow, but hungry, needy.

Charlotte felt Jason's chest lift with a shuddering intake of breath.

"I want to make love," she said against his lips.

Jason went still. His hand, which was sliding up her thigh, stopped at her hip.

"You're sure?"

It was the first time she'd ever made the request, the first time she'd ever initiated their lovemaking.

"Yes."

Lightning briefly brightened the room, shadows frolicked and danced against the walls, followed by the roar of thunder. The bedroom vibrated with sound.

Jason, ever-sensitive to her moods, paused, but she refused to allow any hesitation. She drew his mouth down to hers and they kissed, until Charlotte's whole body seemed to throb with excitement.

Gently Jason removed her nightgown, pulling it over her head. He'd awakened her to an entire world of sensual pleasure in the months since their marriage, a world she wanted to explore *now*.

He hungrily covered her mouth with his

own and her head spun, her nails digging into his back. Abruptly she broke off the kiss, her shoulders heaving. "Jason, please...I want you."

He didn't need any further encouragement....

"Okay, so far?" he asked sometime later.

"Oh, yes," she whispered, smiling her assurance. The pleasure was so keen it was almost beyond bearing.

Lightning flashed and thunder rolled, punctuating their lovemaking. "Jason...oh, Jase," she cried out, her voice a trembling wail of pleasure as her senses caught fire, exploding into a mindless madness. Her body shuddered as she gave herself to the storm, to her husband, to the night.

Afterward, when he, too, had reached completion, they were both panting. Jason gathered her in his arms, and they were silent, words between them unnecessary.

Eventually their breathing steadied.

"I still have trouble believing how good this is," Charlotte whispered. "Making love, I mean."

Jason kissed the crown of her head. "It always has been."

"Not in the beginning."

"It was," he said. "Because you let me try to prove how much I love you."

Charlotte was quiet for a moment as she absorbed his words. Their first attempts at making love, on their honeymoon, had left her frustrated and in tears. She was convinced Jason had made a terrible mistake in marrying her. He wouldn't allow her to criticize herself, though. His patience astonished her and gave her the courage to keep trying.

She'd struggled with her inadequacies, silently condemning herself, but on the seventh night of their stay, they'd broken through the restraints and made beautiful, intoxicating love. Charlotte had wanted everything to be magically different from then on, but that would have been unrealistic. Her fears were unpredictable and continued to be for weeks. But now, four months after their wedding, loving Jason was the most incredible experience of her life.

Tears slipped down Charlotte's cheeks as she recalled the first weeks of their marriage—his gentleness, his unwillingness to give up, his *love*.

"You're crying," he whispered, his lips against her hair.

"You're not supposed to notice."

"But I have. Are you going to tell me why?"

Emotion clogged her throat as she struggled to hold back the tears. "In a minute."

Jason's brow creased with a thoughtful frown. "Is it something that came from your meeting with Bill?"

Bill was her counselor; she saw him twice a week. She shook her head. "You promise you won't laugh?"

"I'll try."

"I'm crying because I'm so happy."

"Happy," Jason repeated slowly. "But if you cry when you're happy, what do you do when you're sad?"

"Cry," she returned with irrefutable logic. "Now aren't you going to ask me *why* I'm so happy?"

"I don't need to. It's obvious."

"It is?"

"Of course. You're married to me."

Charlotte laughed at his mock arrogance. "Carrie cried, too."

"Carrie's *that* happy?"

"It's the reason she's spending the night with a friend. I wanted the evening alone with you."

Jason snickered. "If that's the case, why'd you go to bed at six-thirty?"

"I didn't plan that," she murmured, "but I think it's going to be pretty much the norm for the next few months. I couldn't seem to get enough sleep when I was pregnant with Carrie, either."

"Cute, Charlotte, very cute. You couldn't possibly be—" He stopped cold, his eyes widening.

"It's true," she said, pressing her head to his chest. She smiled as the erratic beat of his heart sounded in her ear.

"How far…?"

"A month."

He shook his head as though in a trance.

"It was inevitable, you know," she told him, happiness spilling from her heart. "How could I not be pregnant? We've been making love for months. And we decided not to use birth control for this very reason."

"Yes, but…"

"When the lovemaking's this good, doesn't it make sense that the result will be equally beautiful?"

Jason kissed her again, his mouth worshipping hers. "I love you so much."

Charlotte sighed and closed her eyes, utterly content. She'd conquered her fears, begun to heal her pain. She'd survived the memories and triumphed over her past.

The future stretched before her, filled with bright promise. She wasn't going to miss a single moment.

* * * * *

The ESSENTIAL COLLECTION

YES! Please send me the *Essential Collection by Debbie Macomber* in Larger Print. This collection begins with 3 FREE books and 2 FREE gifts in the first shipment, and more free gifts will follow! My books will arrive in 8 monthly shipments until I have the entire 51-book *Essential Collection by Debbie Macomber.* I will receive 2 or 3 FREE books in each shipment and I will pay just $4.99 U.S./$5.80 CDN. for each of the other 4 books in each shipment, plus $2.99 for shipping and handling. *If I decide to keep the entire collection, I'll have paid for only 32 books because 19 books are FREE! I understand that by accepting the 3 free books and gifts places me under no obligation to buy anything. I can always return a shipment and cancel at any time. My free books and gifts are mine to keep no matter what I decide.

261 HCN 1446   461 HCN 1446

Name	(PLEASE PRINT)

Address	Apt. #

City	State/Prov.	Zip/Postal Code

Signature (if under 18, a parent or guardian must sign)

Mail to the Harlequin® Reader Service:
IN U.S.A.: P.O. Box 1867, Buffalo, NY 14240-1867
IN CANADA: P.O. Box 609, Fort Erie, Ontario L2A 5X3

* Terms and prices subject to change without notice. Prices do not include applicable taxes. Sales tax applicable in N.Y. Canadian residents will be charged applicable taxes. This offer is limited to one order per household. All orders subject to approval. Credit or debit balances in a customer's account(s) may be offset by any other outstanding balance owed by or to the customer. Please allow 4 to 6 weeks for delivery. Offer available while quantities last. Offer not available to Quebec residents.

Your Privacy—The Harlequin® Reader Service is committed to protecting your privacy. Our Privacy Policy is available online at www.ReaderService.com or upon request from the Harlequin Reader Service.

We make a portion of our mailing list available to reputable third parties that offer products we believe may interest you. If you prefer that we not exchange your name with third parties, or if you wish to clarify or modify your communication preferences, please visit us at www.ReaderService.com/consumerschoice or write to us at Harlequin Reader Service Preference Service, P.O. Box 9062, Buffalo, NY 14269. Include your complete name and address.